This Just In...

BY

KATHRYN SCARBOROUGH

This Just In…

by Kathryn Scarborough Scarboroughbooks.com

Originally Published by Astaea Press

As always:

To Hal and the Three Musketeers. and now to

Trystan

As always:

To Hal and the Three Musketeers. and now to

Trystan

Contents

Chapter One

If my nose ran any more, it would be in a marathon, mumbled Gina, rolling her eyes at her own silly comment. She groped around in the pocket of her ski jacket for a tissue, and found gum wrappers, scraps of paper, a pen, and at last, a piece of tissue that looked like it was used during the Crimean War. With a great sigh, she dabbed at her nose while she waited for her turn to use the ATM.

The icy wind blew through Gina's down----filled parka and she stamped her feet trying to stay warm. She shivered as she stepped through the glass----doored ATM booth, where she was at least out of the wind. Out of the corner of her eye, she glimpsed an ad taped to the inside wall:

For Sale:

Kerosene heater.

Brand----new. Never used.

$35

Call 555----2793

Ask for Mr. Glibmann.

Gina stared at the bit of paper as she blew on her cold fingertips. She rubbed her hands against her backside, trying to get some feeling back into the frozen digits as she re----read the ad.

Her little bungalow on the south side of Huntsville, Alabama, was her pride and joy. She had purchased the house during the summer and had worked on the interior as far as her teacher's salary would stretch. She"d found out, much to her abject misery, that the 40----year----old plus house, she'd purchased, leaked like a sieve, and the heating system was beyond inadequate. No matter where she sat herself down in the little house, she felt a chilling, never ending draft. Hmm, a kerosene heater… it might just be what she needed. It was Saturday. Maybe this Mr. Glibmann was at home.

Completely forgetting about the money she meant to withdraw, Gina left the glass ATM booth, pulled her cell phone from her pocket, and punched in the number from the notice.

"Hello?"

"Hello, are you Mr. Glibmann?"

"And who wants to know if this is Mr. Glibmann?" The voice that answered the phone shook with age and a heavy German accent.

"I'm Gina Thompson, and I'd like to know if the kerosene heater is still for sale?"

"Yes, the heater. You want to look? You can look if you want to. My nephew will be here. I better go to the grocery. If you come now, he'll be here. So, you want to come now?"

Gina pulled the phone away from her ear and looked at it quizzically. Was this guy for real? He sounded like a bad imitation of those old Jewish guys in 1930s movies. Oh well, it takes all kinds. "Oh, yes sir. Tell me where you are and I'll be right over. I'm at the mall near University Drive. Is that far from you?"

"At the mall? At the mall? Always the girls are at the mall." "Mr. Glibmann, I'm hardly a girl and..." Who was this man who sounded, unfortunately, that he was just short of ancient?

Had he perhaps missed all the lectures about the modern woman and how they all hated being called girls?

"Is all right, all right, never mind that. You can come down the University Drive and turn on... "The old man gave a quick set of directions and Gina decided in the middle of the droning voice that she was glad she had her GPS in her glove box. She would just enter the old fellow's address and let Stephen Fry, the voice she'd chosen from the many the GPS had to offer, give her directions. Mr. Fry's lovely English accent intoned, not said, but intoned things like, "There's an exit on the right and that's the very one we want." Or, "To the left if you'd be so lovely." Or, "On to the motorway we go; fabulous." Sometimes, she left the GPS on when she was going to work just so the round dulcet tones of Stephen would make her feel a little less lonely.

She hurried to her car, balancing the phone against her ear. She groped in her purse, but her frozen fingers fumbled with the keys. Gina blew on her hands again as she climbed behind the wheel of her car with the phone still pushed against her ear listening with half her mind to Mr. Glibmann's droning voice give her directions. With the other half, she imagined the blue flame of the kerosene heater dancing about, warming her cold front room as she curled up on the couch reading a book and munching on popcorn. Ah, heaven.

"Sure, sure, come on, come on," said Mr. Glibmann.

"My nephew be here. His name is Kenneth. Kenneth Armstrong. He's an engineer, 32 years old, good---looking guy."

"Sure, Mr. Glibmann," said Gina rolling her eyes at the absurdity of what sounded like matchmaking to a stranger calling about a kerosene heater. "I'll be there in about twenty."

"Uncle Johann…"

"The only time you call me the Johann is when you are upset."

"Look, I am not upset I just cannot stand this incessant match…"

"So you don't want to get married? And my sister?" said the old man, holding his hands up to the ceiling in mock despair. When his uncle talked about his mom, Ken knew he was in it for the long haul. "She's turning over in her grave," he continued, pointing an arthritic finger and wagging it under Ken's nose, "thinking her only child with no children and the poor Uncle Johann left with no one. So, okay, I'll get along fine with no great nephews and nieces. Yes, I will." Uncle Johann ended the tirade by turning his back on his nephew and walking belligerently, if one can walk belligerently, to the coffee pot.

His uncle was always trying to match him up with someone. Johann had heard some woman's voice over the phone and decided she was the "one." Man oh man. The woman probably weighed three hundred pounds and had greasy hair and pimples. Ken decided at that instant that he was going to get away from his uncle's house and not come back until the evening when he checked on Uncle Yo, as he liked to call him, before he turned in for the night.

"Uncle Yo, I got to go, see you later," called Ken. He waved, climbed into his car, and backed out of the driveway. He watched Uncle Yo until he had turned the corner. But his uncle had never lost that disgruntled look.

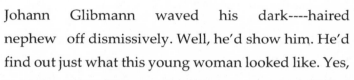

Johann Glibmann waved his dark----haired nephew off dismissively. Well, he'd show him. He'd find out just what this young woman looked like. Yes, he'd show him. He wasn't getting any younger. If Ken wouldn't go out and look for a woman, then he, Johann, would do it for him. He felt it in his bones: the woman coming over was the one.

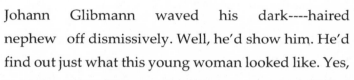

Gina drove slowly down the sycamore----lined street, looking at the house numbers she'd scribbled on the tiny scrap of paper as she listened to Stephen Fry's voice coming through her GPS. "Yes, now, after three hundred yards..."

One ear was listening to the directions given by the GPS while her mind turned over all she knew about kerosene heaters. She assumed they could be dangerous; raw fuel, wooden floors, and fumes, all of those bits of data didn't mix well. But she supposed anything could be dangerous if one didn't use it correctly. She'd ask her dad to buy her a carbon monoxide detector. Gina's mind flashed a picture of dead cartoon fish with crosses for eyes. Maybe she'd look like that in the morning.

"Oh, Gina, cool it. You don't know if you even want the thing or not." She was always getting ahead of herself. Time to slow down and act like the grown up, she'd been for a long, long time.

Just then, Steven Fry's voice chortled, "You have reached your destination, congratulations...I think I may be falling in love with you." Gina always tried to turn off the GPS before she could hear that silliness. She wasn't quick enough with the off button today. Stephen intoning those words always felt like he was rubbing it in somehow. She couldn't remember when or if that had been said to her. Sigh...enough already!

The small bungalow, in the style of those built in the city right after WWII, hadn't been hard to find. Gingerbread----adorned flower boxes were on every front window, and the glass storm door sparkled in the late afternoon sun. Driving slowly up the drive, Gina noted the tidiness and organization of the small house. If the heater was in as half good order as the property, she'd have a bargain.

"Hello, is anyone here?" she called. She walked toward an old----fashioned, red, wooden----framed door with a brightly polished brass doorknob. A note was taped to the front:

Had to go out.

The heater is in the back, so you take a look. If you still want, come again at 7:30.

7:30? 7:30? The old guy's got to be kidding. That little blue flame of warmth and coziness went out in Gina's imagination with an almost audible "poof." She stifled her irritation and marched toward the back of the house. The heater sat on the back stoop, clean and shiny and decidedly brand----new.

"Gosh, this thing looks great. I'll bring Andy over tonight and he can help me check it out," she muttered to herself. Her twin brother, Andy, would be terribly put out about missing whatever he was missing on a Saturday night, but that was just tough. What were brothers for anyway? And besides, if one asked the other to do something, 'no' was never said. But, Gina didn't want to push her luck; maybe he'd say 'no' today.

While Gina examined the heater, Johann quietly watched from behind the kitchen door.

"A red----head. Wahoo!"

Ken Armstrong pushed the computer sound card into his CPU with a vengeance. His Uncle Yo could get to him quicker than anyone. He supposed that was what relatives were for. Bah humbug. Ken had been burned one too many times. The last relationship he had with a woman, a sure thing, he thought, had been a complete disaster. He found the capricious woman had been more interested in his boss. Talk about finding out the hard way, he'd walked in on the two of them at a party. Everyone else at the party had seen the whole sordid scene too. It had been so humiliating…

Uncle Yo would just have to suffer. His matchmaking

could go on to the back burner for a while, and just stay there, until, well, Ken wasn't exactly sure when he'd be ready to make a move to settle down.

Ken sighed as he looked up at the clock. Oh man, it was 6:30 already. He would have to go to Uncle Yo's soon and make sure he wasn't burning down the house cooking his famous whatever he was cooking tonight.

"Listen to me, please. Just take a look at it for me, will you?"

"I'm supposed to meet Rachel at 7:30, okay?"

"Andy, how long does it take to check out a kerosene heater?"

"All right, all right, but can we hurry? I'll follow you in my car, that way I'll save some time."

"Oh, joy, my hero, Sir Andrew," Gina said.

"Complain, complain. I told you not to buy that leaky old rat trap of a house. You need to listen to your older and wiser brother," Andy teased.

"Older? Older?"

"Well, yes, by two minutes, I believe," said Andy. "Oh, brother, I can't believe you love bringing that up."

Driving in tandem, they reached the little bungalow on the south side of Huntsville in record time. Gina rang the bell and a beaming, bent up, white----haired old man with bushes for eyebrows, opened the door so quickly Gina was sure he'd been watching out for her.

"Come in, come in. It is so good to see you. I am Johann Glibmann and this, this…" The old man turned. "Where are you, Ken, Kenneth?"

Mr. Glibmann walked to the back of the house looking for someone named Ken as Gina felt the tension coming from Andy and his loud mental message, "Hurry up."

"Mr. Glibmann, would you mind terribly showing us the heater? My brother has to go soon."

"Your brother, your brother, of course, I should've seen it right away. You look so much alike."

"Well, we're twins you see, and…"

"Twins! I can't believe it!" Johann rattled on and on and on and Gina felt her head begin to spin. Perhaps she had walked through the looking glass, and she was somewhere in Wonderland with a heater behind every door. The scenario flashed through her mind:

"This just in…. local schoolteacher talked to death by old German man… film… at 11."

Gina held up her hand. "Mr. Glibmann, might we see the heater, sir?" She was, after all, a high school teacher and knew how and when to gain order from chaos.

"Why sure, why sure, I bring you to it, all right. Kenneth, Kenneth," the old man called. "Where are you?"

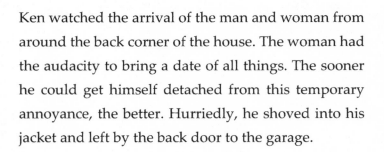

Ken watched the arrival of the man and woman from around the back corner of the house. The woman had the audacity to bring a date of all things. The sooner he could get himself detached from this temporary annoyance, the better. Hurriedly, he shoved into his jacket and left by the back door to the garage.

He heard his uncle calling, but pretended not to.

13

Maybe they would go away. No such luck. He could hear the entire entourage approaching down the gravel path. The door creaked open and Ken felt his jaw drop in surprise as one intensely beautiful woman walked into the workshop. The woman's chocolate----brown eyes were so dark that they looked like mirrors with an even darker center. He knew if he looked too long, he'd drown in them. Her perfectly heart----shaped face was framed by an abundance of auburn hair, and she was petite. He thought the top of her head might just clear his chin and…

———————————•◦●●●◦•———————————

Gina and Andy followed the old man out his back door and down a crunchy gravel path to a rickety old garage that must've been a workshop of some sort. And there at the workbench sat a man, and what a man.

He was tall, she thought. Maybe over 6 feet and lanky and dark. His hair was wavy and cascaded across his forehead and over his collar. His angular face, with high well----defined cheekbones and a square rugged chin, made her think of the well----known painting of

St. George slaying the dragon. But the clincher was his eyes. They were the most vividly colored eyes she'd ever seen. They were a violet----blue and they were looking at Gina right now with an indescribable emotion.

The old man's babbling voice intruded on her lustful thoughts. "Kenneth, where have you been?"

"Right here, Uncle Yo."

"Yes, so, this is Gina Thompson and her brother Andy. They are twins, do you believe it? I was just telling her…"

Ken barely registered his uncle's babbling over the roar of his own brain. So the guy was her brother. Well that was all right then…He applied the brakes to his runaway thoughts. No, no, no. I will not become involved with another woman that my uncle has set up for me.

Ken realized he was staring rudely at the woman. "Huh?

Did you say something Uncle Yo?"

"Show the brother the heater, Kenneth."

15

"Yeah, I'll do it right now." Ken led the way to the workbench where the heater sat in all its shiny glory. He explained the lighting mechanism, the safety features, and explained to them about the BTUs and heating capability. He watched as Gina and Andy nodded their heads at precisely the same instance and netted their brows at exactly the same moment in exactly the same way. Uncanny. Ken took a big breath to clear his mind and concentrate on his task as he turned to Gina. "Would you like to buy the heater?"

"Oh yes, I'd love it. My house gets awfully cold."

Gina pulled some bills from her wallet and then turned to Andy as if in afterthought. "What do you think?"

Andy consulted his watch. "I think I have to meet Rachel in 15 minutes and I think the heater is fine. Leave it here. I'll pick it up tomorrow and take it to your place."

"Tomorrow?" Gina's face fell. The cozy, little blue flame in her imagination went out again. Rats.

"Nah, nah. Kenneth will carry it for you. Right, Ken? Yes, yes, he will carry it for you in his car to your home, and show you how to light it," the old man said.

"Mr. Glibmann, I can't impose." The phrase rushed out of Gina in one breath. The last thing she wanted was this tall good---- looking man to invade her house. She'd had about enough of that, thank you very much. That last boyfriend of hers practically cured her of men for good. Gina snuck a peek at him out of the corner of her eye. Well, maybe.

"Hey, that's great," said Andy. "That will be terrific if you could help my sister, and I'll return the favor someday." He ducked his head quickly to peck Gina on the cheek before he sprinted towards his car with a hasty wave of his hand. "Bye, Sis."

The rapid chain of events had Ken's jaw dropping in surprise while Gina's face crumbled. How could Andy leave her and, more importantly, how could she get herself entrenched with this crazy old man and this great----looking young man, all for the want of a heater?

"Now, now, now, you come and have a cup of tea with me and Ken will put the heater in your car."

This whole situation was getting out of control. Andy had left her with a bunch of strangers, and one of them was so gorgeous she felt like she'd fall down and kiss his feet if she didn't watch herself.

Yes, yes, pay attention to me. Look at me, with those gorgeous blue eyes, were Gina's thoughts.

Mr. Glibmann led her back into the house and seated her at a built----in bench that ran across the back wall of his kitchen. She looked around intently at the long dinette table in front of the bench. It looked like scrubbed wood—very, very scrubbed wood—and hand----polished.

"Really, Mr. Glibmann, you needn't give me any refreshments, and here is the money for the heater."

Gina laid the bills on the table as she looked around the cozy little kitchen with frank curiosity. She was still fixing her little bungalow up as her budget allowed. Before long her home would be completely finished to her satisfaction, but until then, she got great ideas from looking at other homes.

Mr. Glibmann set a cup of tea in front of her along with a little plate of anise cookies. The aroma from the small white pastries, which had just been pulled from a still----warm oven, wafted up and made her mouth water. She closed her eyes and savored the first bite of her cookie, while her fertile mind imagined Ken lifting the heavy heater and putting it in his car.

Gina shook her head to clear the buzzing in her ears and concentrated on the spice rack next to the stove. It had to be hand---- carved with a custom finish. She drew her hands across the table, feeling the raised grain of the wood, subtle but distinct, under her fingers. It must be handmade as well, just like the cornices above the window that looked out over the sink.

"You have a lovely home, Mr. Glibmann." And a lovely nephew, too, she thought.

"Oh, thank you, my dear. Me, I got two thumbs. I couldn't even find a jar of nails. My nephew, he built all this for me when he was in college. He went to MIT, but he lived with me during the vacations. His parents died when he was young."

"Oh, that's sad."

"Yes, Kenneth's mother was my sister. She came here to stay with me after the war and she met Ken's father who worked with me at Marshall Space Flight Center. She was more than 15sens years younger than me. During the war, she stayed with our grandparents.

But, they died in the bombing of our village. We lived near Freiburg in the Black Forest, near the Rhine River."

Gina thought of her own crazy, many times dysfunctional family. She knew how chaotic her brothers and sisters, parents, aunts and uncles, grandparents, and all the various and sundry cousins could be. It would be very strange and it would be very unhappy to be without anyone in an extended family and living with only one old man.

Her mind went back to the last time she'd spent a night with her family.

"Jeffy, slow down!"

"Janice, get him to stop running in the house," Gina called out.

"Aunt Gina, he's fine," her sister had called from the kitchen where she was talking to their mother.

"Spoiled rotten kid," Gina had muttered, trying to duck around Jeffy as he tore through the living room. "JANICE, he's going to run into something and get hurt." Janice did not respond.

Gina tried to side step her nephew hurtling through

the living room. It looked like he was aiming a peanut butter and jelly sandwich right at her.

"Brooooooom," he'd yelled as he'd careened around the coffee table and ran smack into her, grinding the peanut butter all down the front of her white lamb's wool tunic. Gina hollered in disbelief at the mess made of her tunic. She glared at Jeffy and was on the verge of throttling him. She growled and made a move to grab the little so and so when she saw the little smirk he gave her.

"Janice, he's done it again, he's ruined my tunic. Oh, how can you just let him run around like an out of control barbarian?"

Of course Jeffy had made crocodile tears and 'mama' had come to his rescue, petting him as she scowling at Gina.

Her niece had wailed; not whined, but wailed, the entire time Gina had been at her parent's and her head was still pounding with it.

Gina thought that a quiet life would be so nice. But, maybe being without a family was something else again. How much worse would it be to come to terms with your entire family dying in a war? That would be very hard to take.

Her teaching job could be as nerve racking as any, probably more so than many, and teaching in a high school could really leave one's ears ringing. But at least she her students, no matter how infuriating they sometimes got could go home and weren't in danger of getting shot by some Russian or Nazi.

In the middle of Mr. Glibmann's droning voice and Gina's musings, the back door opened and in walked Sir Gala… hmm. He gave her a staring look, as though he wasn't sure what to make of her. She, on the other hand, could not believe this gorgeous hunk of man was running around unattached. Or was he?

Gina, do you really need to know if the man is unattached? Do you really care?

Yes!

Gina, you are going to have to cool it or the buzzing in your ears may turn into bells… bells tolling your ultimate doom.

"We can go whenever you're ready," Ken said making his way to the sink to wash his hands.

"Sure." Gina took another sip of her tea, shrugged

into her jacket, and walked quickly to the front door. It occurred to her then that Ken was going to follow her home in his car. Holy Moly, what if the guy was a serial killer or a torturer of women and she was going to lead him to her home?

Oh, Gina, cool it. How could anybody, so gorgeous be anything but gorgeous? Yeah, but now I remember; wasn't Ted Bundy, the man everyone thought was so nice, gorgeous too?

Gina shivered as she walked out the door.

With a wave to Mr. Glibmann, she climbed into her dark green four----door sedan to lead the way up the mountain to her little bungalow.

She kept looking in her rearview mirror, making sure she hadn't dreamed the whole scenario.

She came to the left----hand turn that wound up Monte Sano Mountain, and waited for oncoming traffic. She hated this turn, the people coming down the steep grade acted like they were on a flat piece of beach and usually whizzed by as though the forty----five degree down angle and the often----slippery roads were nothing to worry about. Dispassionate drivers were bound to get one killed quicker than someone paying attention.

At last she got the green light, and her sedan and Ken's car squeezed through the turn. For the next two miles driving slowly up the curvy mountain road, Gina tried to think of creative lesson plans for her astronomy class of advanced placement seniors, and not about the Jeep hot on her tail.

She had looked for houses in this part of town because of its proximity to the von Braun Planetarium. She had ingratiated herself with the planetarium staff and had gotten in to do a bit of research now and again.

Gina rolled into her driveway at last. She was relieved the motion sensors above the garage doors that Andy had put in turned the lights on without a hitch.

She opened the door with the remote and pulled in, leaving enough room for Ken to bring the heater through the inside door that led into the kitchen from the garage.

Ken lugged the heater in, uncomfortably squeezing past her as she held open the door and on their contact, Gina felt a tingling like the static shock she got from touching metal on dry winter days.

Come on Thompson. There's no such thing as a true chemically induced physical attraction. No love at first sight, none of that stuff. You're a scientist, remember?

Colleen, Gina's yellow Labrador retriever, bounded up to her with a happy bark. Ken stopped to let Colleen give him the once over with her nose before she let him pass into the house without so much as a peep.

Gina knit her brow in surprise. Colleen never let anyone, especially a man, through the door without a good going over with her nose and sometimes a growl. She let Ken in with hardly a rumble and bumped her tail merrily against his leg.

Ken frowned slightly at the dog as he lugged in the heater, but said not a word until he stood in the center of the small living room.

"Where do you want it?"

"I've been thinking about that, how about if I put it on this plant stand with the wheels?"

"No, it's made of wood."

"Oh, yeah." Okay, she thought, not thinking straight.

Gina hurried into the kitchen, and brought back the biggest metal tray she could find and plopped it down into the center of the room.

"Are you sure this is where you want it? The thing weighs about sixty pounds." Ken waited for a beat for Gina's response and then gratefully put the heater down with a thump, straightened up, and looked around curiously for a second before bending down nose to nose with Colleen.

"Hey girl," he said as he rubbed her behind the ears. "How do you know she's a girl?"

"Too good----looking to be a boy."

Chapter Two

He wasn't sure why, but Ken thought the house would be filled with crocheted doilies and tie----dyed pillows. What he did see surprised him very much; not only was this woman a beauty, but Gina was obviously a brain.

The alcove that would have been the previous owners' tiny dining room was now an office stuffed to the brim with serious looking equipment. The high----powered computer was fitted with two monitors and an ultra----cool cordless keyboard, mouse, and speakers. Star charts were plastered on the wall opposite the computer and a book of astronomical data lay open next to the monitor. The table top was littered from bottom to top with papers, graphs, and books, as were the coffee table and couch. Stacks of what looked like test papers lay across the floor in semi----neat piles.

Ken's all too candid scrutiny left Gina a bit flustered. Yeah, well, the place was a mess. It was clean, but she just had tons of work to do and that work usually ended up on the floor until she could figure out what to do with it.

Another headline flashed through Gina's mind:

"This just in...Teacher arrested by neat and tidy police.

Gina shook her head. Her mind worked like...well, who knew what her mind worked like? She hoped it worked like a pragmatic scientist....NOT.

She hoped someday to eradicate the ever present movie/TV camera in her head. That imagined camera followed her around incessantly.

"Oh, sorry," she mumbled, feeling her face flush. "I usually have this screen up so no one has to see the office." Gina quickly took a standing screen and stretched it across the opening to the area. At least he would only be able to see all the other junk.

Ken made one slow turn, taking in the overstuffed couch, the flounced curtains, and the mahogany table with the Queen Ann legs. The facing wall was painted a pretty mauve that picked up the tones in the afghan and flowered print on the overstuffed chair. There were flowers and plants in every nook and cranny. The room looked like what Ken imagined an English tearoom might...minus all the books and papers, of course. It was very homey, comfortable... and cold. He absently rubbed Colleen's ears before chafing his hands together.

"What kind of heat do you have here?"

"Electric. All electric. It must've been one of the first kinds of houses that was all electric. Someone put in a heat pump 15 years ago or so. They don't work too well when the temp gets below freezing. I think the high was twenty----nine today. Brr. And mine doesn't seem to work, regardless."

"This heater will probably blow you out of here. If you have a little fan you could push some of the hot air to the back."

"That's an idea."

———————————•◦●◦•———————————

. A very hunky guy stood in the middle of her living room, just standing there with open and frank curiosity that was a bit daunting, making Gina feel a little self----conscious

Gina took a peek at those wide shoulders. He was so wide in the chest that his jacket stretched across his back and looked like it might pop as Ken bent down to fiddle with the heater. She felt herself staring, trying very hard not to look at the area south of his waist...and for just that moment, it didn't seem quite so cold in the little house.

Gina looked at Colleen in an effort to look somewhere besides...and saw that Colleen was actually preening for Ken. How come her faithful dog with such a pushover? Despite Coleen's non---- human, color blind eye sight, Gina knew her dog thought Ken was gorgeous.

"You'll have to get someone to help you move the heater if you want it somewhere else," said Ken as he looked up from his bent over position. As he stood, she did a double take when his eyes riveted into hers. It was as though he was trying to look inside her head. Gina willed herself not to blush and turned around and sat quickly on the couch.

He cleared his throat roughly and then bent again to his task. He looked about the room for a moment and then up at Gina and beckoned her to watch the lighting procedure. She got up from the couch and leaned over, intently listening to the instructions.

"I think that it's in a good location. Now, this is how you start it, you lift up this little lever and...

Gina bent her head down to look at the lighting mechanism as Ken looked up and whack! They knocked heads.

"Oh my God you've got a hard head," said Gina as she collapsed on the couch clutching at her temple and rubbing it hard.

Ken rubbed his forehead vigorously noting that, for a moment, he really did see stars, and not the ones plastered all over the walls of Gina's office.

"Yeah, well, I'm half German. You know what they say about German heads... I've been informed that they are the absolute thickest in all of Europe."

Gina cringed as a sizeable bump began to show on Ken's forehead.

"Do you want some ice for that?" Gina asked as she reached over to put her fingers lightly against the sizeable bump showing up on Ken's forehead. Ken felt a subtle electric current pass between the two of them when her warm hand touched him. Ken took her hand and held it for a moment and looked deeply into her eyes.

"You've got the neatest eyes," he murmured almost too softly for her to hear. "I think I could look into them forever."

Ken let her fingers drop and looked embarrassed. Then he smiled at her. "No, I'll just stand in the cold for a minute when I leave. It's about eighteen degrees out there. At least as cold as any ice you may have." He looked around the room in an obvious attempt to get the conversation back under control.

"Looks like you're working on a project. Are you gleaning information from Marshall Space Flight

Center?" he asked. He abruptly moved the screen to the office to one side, looking with interest at the star charts and equations Gina had doodled on a pad of graph paper, but drew his mind back to the task at hand before he looked up. "I'll tell you what; I'll give you my e----mail and if you have any problems with the heater, just drop me a line." He smiled down at her and Gina decided that the room was heating up agreeably even though the heater had not yet been turned on.

"Why don't you give me your cell number, too, in case it looks as though the thing's about to blow up? I'll be able to get in touch with you a little faster," suggested Gina.

"Sure," he chuckled. "Say," said Ken, gesturing to Gina's computer. "What are all these star charts here? Are you a hobbyist, an astronomer? Do you work at Marshall?"

"No, I teach astronomy to advanced placement seniors at Grissom High School in the city. I have my masters in physical science, not astronomy, and it would really be nice if I knew what I was talking about in class," she said with a little rueful smile.

Ken nodded and then gave her the scrap of paper with his number and email. He abruptly turned and busied himself with lighting the heater. The need to distance himself from this beautiful, intelligent woman before he fell on his face and embarrassed himself so completely he wouldn't be able to look in the mirror and shave tomorrow became paramount. He couldn't even see a woman to her home without panting after her like some... Enough already. No more women, remember, Armstrong?

"What do you do?" asked Gina, warming her hands over the heater. The heater was pumping out a steady stream of warmth, and the cold in the room began to slowly dissipate. It may take a while, but she felt like she could at last thaw out.

Ken watched her smile for just a moment and then, feeling like that panting beast again, turned and looked out the window. "I work over at Marshall Space Flight Center."

"At NASA?" Gina's ears perked up. Was that cool or what? The goings on at Marshall had been the center of her sphere of interest for quite a while. "What you do?"

"Oh, I'm an engineer." "What kind of engineer?" "Um, astrophysical." "Okay, I'm impressed."

"Don't be," he said. He pulled his gloves out of his pocket and looked down at his shoes. "Well, I gotta go. So, there's the number." Ken pointed to the scrap of paper he'd written on lying on the corner of Gina's desk. He picked up the scrap and laid it in the center of the book of astronomical data Gina had lain open. "Hope everything works out all right."

"Thanks for everything." Gina's words bounced off the door as it thudded to a close. The man could not wait to make a very hurried exit. She heard his jeep start and the sound of the car backing out of the drive and turning into the street. She listened as the sound of the engine faded away. Then all she heard was the hiss of the kerosene burning gently in the heater. Gina felt a little depressed. Gee, I wish he'd stayed longer, she thought.

She collapsed happily on the couch, feeling the

warmth penetrate her many layers of clothing. Colleen nudged her nose into Gina's hand, trying to get her to rub her head. The blue flame danced and jumped and slowly became a pair of violet----blue eyes.

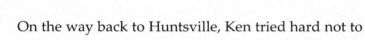

On the way back to Huntsville, Ken tried hard not to think of a pair of chocolate brown eyes that stabbed at the tiny crack in the shield around his heart.

His parents' loving relationship crowded his thoughts. His mother had come to live with her only living relative, Uncle Yo, in Huntsville after the Second World War. She was barely a teenager and had no one besides her brother Johann.

His parents had met and had what Ken remembered as a loving marriage. Why couldn't he find a relationship that would last? Well, if you could answer that one…

His father had died when Ken was eleven and his mother had passed away during his senior year of high school.

He'd been living with or around Uncle Yo ever since.

The old man could be such a pain, especially now that he thought Ken needed to be married and have a family of his own.

Ken sat on his couch in his West Huntsville apartment with an ice pack on the particularly large bump on his forehead.

His cat, Butch, jumped without ceremony or warning on his head at precisely the moment his phone rang.

"Hey, Butch, give us a break, okay?" he said as he dumped the cat on the floor. He glanced at the clock. 10:15! It could only be Uncle Yo. His crotchety old uncle never lets up.

"Hello," Ken growled into the receiver. "So, and, did you get to Gina's house?" "Yes, Uncle Yo, I got to Gina's house." "So, tell me."

"So what do you want me to tell you? She's a brain. She teaches astronomy to advanced placement seniors at Grissom High School and her office looks like an observatory minus the telescope. As a matter of fact, she lives just a few miles from the Von Braun Planetarium."

"But this is wonderful. What a package, brains and beauty," intoned the old man rapturously.

"Uncle Yo, I'm not interested in women at the moment, and—"

"Not interested in women? What? You interested in men?

Listen, my boy, it ain't over till it's over. I'm still looking around." "Uncle Yo, you?"

"Yes, me. What you think I'm dead already? There is a nice little woman I'm seeing at the senior center and—"

"Uncle Yo, you're seeing a woman?" The news pleased Ken immensely. His uncle had been alone too much and for too long.

"Yes, what you think? I spend my days planning meals for you and cleaning this already clean house?"

Ken scratched his head, trying to imagine his uncle in a romantic liaison, kissing a tottering old woman, but Uncle Yo's gruff voice stopped his thoughts right there...thank goodness.

"So, when are you going to see her again?"

"Uncle Yo, I don't know. I gave her my phone number and my e----mail address so she could contact me in case there was trouble with the heater. I have no idea if she will even try. I don't think I told you about Rachel, did I?" Maybe if he told his uncle about his last disastrous relationship, he'd lighten up.

"You mean that girl with the legs that look like a chicken's?" "Her legs did not 'look like a chicken's,' Uncle Yo, and—" "Nah, nah, I remember, she was scrawny, like a chicken.

Now this girl Gina—"

"Look, Uncle Yo, I don't know anything about this girl Gina, but I will tell you that 'burned once, twice shy'. Right now, I've had it with women and I want a rest."

"So, you want to rest, do you? So, okay, I'll give you some room, no more pushing, goodnight."

"Yeah, right, no more pushing," Ken said into the buzzing receiver. "Like the sun won't rise again." He snorted. Ken hoisted Butch up onto his lap and absently rubbed him behind the ears. He sat lost in thought as Butch's purr rumbled in his lap. Lost in a pair of dark brown eyes.

———————•••••———————

Johann hung up the phone and rubbed his hands together gleefully. "Wahoo, an astronomer. I'll just see what I can do to hurry this thing along. I ain't getting any younger, waiting for my nephew to produce some brilliant, redheaded little kinder."

———————•••••———————

Gina was still smiling on Monday at the lovely, quiet, warm Sunday she'd had in her own little house. Several times this winter she'd been forced out of her little bungalow and sought the warmth of her parents' or Andy's home. If she went to Andy's, she had to put up with dirty dishes, beer bottles, and nasty bathrooms until, completely disgusted, she'd break down and clean his apartment for him.

If she went to her parents' very nice house in the neighboring town of Madison, she had to listen to her niece wail.

Well, to be completely fair, she supposed if her parents had broken up, and she had to live with her grandparents when she was seven, she'd wail too.

40

She was glad she taught high school. Dealing with students, nieces and nephews under the age of ten could really be a pain.

And then she thought of Ken. Matter of fact, it was getting hard to avoid thinking about him every second. What a man, all beauty and astrophysical engineering, too. Be still my heart, Gina thought.

Gina frowned as she catalogued the last few men of which she had the misfortune of just being around.

One fat, old football coach came into her office constantly and tried to stroke her hair. She'd told him at least three times that she wasn't interested. Obviously, the guy had gotten hit in the head with a football too many times and would not get the message. One day, not long after she'd started teaching at Grissom, the coach had come into her office and perched himself on the edge of her desk. He started talking like he was in love with the sound of his own voice. Never taking her gaze off his face, Gina pulled open the elastic waistband of his gym pants, and poured an ice cold cola down them. The coach jumped up screaming and ran out of her office like a banshee was after him.

41

The word had spread, after that, and only a few lechers hung around her office... until, that is, the new assistant band director, Ralph Johnson. That episode still made her blush all the way to the tops of her socks.

Ralph had been wonderful and romantic. He wrote her notes and left roses and cologne on her desk. It was all so perfect...until she'd found out, while she was kissing him in the supply room.

That day he'd lifted her onto a table in the supply room and began kissing her, nuzzling her neck and biting her lips and taking all sorts of liberties, till she thought she would absolutely lose it.

She'd pulled him closer and closer, and began wrapping her legs around his waist, when one of the secretaries, an older woman who was a friend of her mother's and whom she'd known her whole life, walked in on them. Gina never knew how much Betty had seen in the dark room, as she hurriedly hopped down off the table.

"Why, Mr. Johnson," Betty had crooned, after she'd turned on the lights and looked at the two of them for one painful moment. "And Gina, how is that class coming?"

"Fine, ma'am."

"Well, that's wonderful, and Mr. Johnson, how is that new baby of yours, and your wife? When will she and your children be joining you from Montgomery? I received such a nice thank you from her when we sent the flowers to the hospital after she had the baby. She must be a lovely woman. And how old is the baby, three weeks?"

"Um, yes."

Gina had felt all the color drain from her face. Looking neither right nor left, she'd pushed past Betty and left the room without saying a word.

Later that afternoon, when all of the one hundred twenty teachers and most of the staff had gone home, Gina plotted her revenge.

Betty wouldn't tell anyone. Her mother's friend had probably seen her go into the closet with the lecher and tried to warn Gina without being too obvious.

Gina left her office, and found one of the janitors she knew.

She made up an elaborate story about something and the janitor unlocked the band room and Ralph's office for her. Gina knew she was alone in that part of the building, so she took her time with her plan. From the chemistry lab, she'd brought a bottle of a non----toxic, very smelly, very nasty chemical in liquid form.

Ralph, who played woodwinds and was the woodwind instructor, housed all the oboe and clarinet reeds in his office.

Gina pulled out Ralph's personal instruments and soaked the mouthpieces and reeds in the chemical. As she'd waited for the chemical to soak into the wood, she looked around in his desk. There were love notes and bottles of cologne addressed to two first---- year teachers that Gina was vaguely acquainted with. She took out the notes and scribbled in red across them, "He's married and has a three----week----old baby." Then she deposited them and the cologne in her purse.

Some five minutes later, she turned on the fan to dispel any odor, patted the reeds and mouthpieces very lightly with a paper towel, returned them to their

44

proper places, and left the office, making sure the door locked behind her.

On her way out the building, she deposited the notes in the teachers' mailboxes, and smiled a smug smile.

In the teachers' lunchroom the next day, Ralph had what looked like the beginnings of a black eye. It couldn't have happened to a nicer guy.

Gina decided after playing that particular rerun of her most embarrassing moments since adulthood, she would decidedly not pursue this guy Ken. I mean, who has the stamina to put up with men?

Gina's mind continued to rewind the past until she slipped into a particularly sublime daydream of knights, their armor glinting in the sun, jousting in a dusty field. A puff of wind ruffled the most handsome knight's dark, wavy hair. But, it wasn't a puff of wind; it was the door to her office opening.

"Miss Thompson?"

Gina snapped out of the daydream in a flash. "Yes?"

Standing by her desk were two of the brightest seniors in her astronomy class, watching her frown. Jimmy Henderson and Renee Butterfield were going together, but they were still bright enough to be able to share assignments and not walk on each other's toes.

"We thought up a project and would like your okay with it." "I'm listening."

"Could we go over to Marshall Space Flight Center and do some research on the Mars Probe, just enough to write a paper on how it works and how it can be recycled in the future? Nothing too involved."

"Nothing too involved, huh? Sounds pretty involved to me. And how do you plan to go over to NASA anyway? One of your dads or uncles or aunts work there?"

"No, ma'am. We were hoping you could help us with that part. Surely you know someone over there? Doesn't your dad work at Marshall Space Flight Center?"

"No. My dad works at the University in the meteorological department, nothing whatever to do with anything past our atmosphere. Maybe I can come up with something. Keep your fingers crossed," said Gina. It was time for her next class and she had to hustle herself into her classroom.

Her Earth Science class settled themselves in the room, but Gina's mind was doing cartwheels about Ken Armstrong. Would he help her students? And just maybe... Well, she'd see about that.

First, though, she was going to have to do a little research on the man. And where do you do research? At the source, of course. She would not, she vowed, move so much as her little toe in the direction of Ken Armstrong until she found out everything she could about him. He was probably just like the rest of them. To be completely fair, she just had to find out. Was he worth it?

Mr. Glibmann was going to get a visit from her today at approximately 3:30 p.m., and she was going to glean every bit of information she could out of the old man.

She would just have to try to do it without being too obvious.

Ken sat at his desk at the Marshall Space Flight Center just daydreaming. One of his buddies waved a sheaf of computer printouts somewhere in the vicinity of his nose.

"Now look, Ken, we've got to make sure this thing is going to work. Have you double----checked your figures on this?"

"Tom, what did you say?" Ken looked up and stared at the man. Oh man, he'd forgotten he was there. Ken had been daydreaming again. About Gina. Something he'd been doing for two days now and it was about time he stopped. No matter what he was doing: eating, working out, laundry, cleaning, or at work, thoughts of Gina would intrude and keep him from completing his tasks.

Good grief! He had to stop this. He'd been done to, done in, and done out by women. If he tried, he couldn't think of one relationship that he'd had that had gone right. His heart had a wall around it that he had put there himself and mortared brick by brick. Not one little crack was open to the world. Not one little crack.

Well, maybe one.

•••●●●••

Chapter Three

From: Gina Tho**mpson<starlady@triad.lr.net**> To: Ken Armstrong< **kenarm@triang.al.net**> Subject: Heater/ trip to…

Dear Ken,

Many thanks for setting up and lighting the heater. It runs great and I'm sure all 35,000 BTUs were pumping out last Saturday night and Sunday. You were right, the heat can about blow you out of here. I hope you will be gratified to know that this old schoolmarm is avoiding frostbite for the time being. On to other matters… I have two brilliant young students, Jimmy Anderson and Renee Butterfield, who would like very much to meet you, for research purposes you understand. They have chosen to do a paper on the future of the Mars Probe.

Have you at your disposal any information they might use?

I would think that it may take only a short amount of your time. If the paper is accepted, the two may earn three credit hours for a two hundred level college course.

Well, think about it. My phone is 555----5544. Gina

Gina looked at the computer screen and re----read her email once again and, despite herself, a little sigh escaped her.

She'd spent the afternoon with Mr. Glibmann, trying to understand what she hoped to gain by going all the way across town to see him. Mr. Glibmann's eyes were exactly the same color as Ken's, and every time she looked into Johann Glibmann's face, she felt a shiver.

Mr. Glibmann spoke of Ken as a nice, unattached (which was a plus) man, good to old people, and dogs loved him. It should not be a difficult decision for Gina to see that Ken might just be okay to go date. To just go out with. Who had the energy for a serious relationship? Things that were too good to be true usually were. She sat back from the computer. She'd wait and see how he responded after he'd read her e----mail. If Ken was as good as she thought he was, then just maybe he'd think about helping her very deserving students, and then there just might be the plus of a possible date.

During the course of the afternoon that she'd spent with Johann, Gina had learned more than she had hoped to. Not too much gushing about the wonderful nephew, no baby pictures poised on the bearskin rug, no teething rings, none of the malarkey that grandparents could usually not avoid. Johann was clever, Gina thought, very clever, and it was obvious he was pumping Gina for information too.

Gina had helped herself to another little anise cookie while she thought happily of Ken and the possibilities and Johann bragged about Ken's enormous responsibility at Marshall Space Flight Center.

"And he likes to go camping, you know, the whole schlemiel when you hike up the mountain, and chop your own wood, the whole thing. The outdoors is just his ticket," the old man had practically chortled. The two stopped talking and just sat. A little smile tugged at the corners of his mouth, not quite there, but not quite absent either.

"I like camping and fishing," Gina said as she tried to break the spell that had settled over the room. "But my house is so cold now, it spoils it when I have to fight old man winter outside as well."

"Why don't you fix it already?"

"Because it will cost ten thousand six hundred and ninety four dollars and some odd cents." "Ouch. So you need everything replaced, huh?"

"That's right, and I have neither the time nor stamina to work a second job. Maybe during the summer I can be a lifeguard at the water park. I hear they make a whopping ten bucks an hour.

"Say, Mr. Glibmann, do you think Ken would help my students with a project?"

"Well, why don't you tell me the whole thing?" said Mr. Glibmann, his eyes twinkling. "You can count on me, you know. I know him best of anyone. You just tell Johann what you want and I get it from that rascally boy."

Gina smiled and sipped her tea, and told Johann about her advanced placement students and their paper. There was a lot to think about.

"Mr. Glibmann, do you have family still living in Germany?" Gina changed the subject abruptly. Mr. Glibmann had been fishing for information about her during their short time together. Now, maybe she could find some more information out about his family. Were there only he and Ken? Did he have anyone in the world, but his nephew?

"Oh, no, no, that place isn't there anymore."

"You mean the whole town?" Gina asked. She was dumbfounded. As an American, she was not used to hearing about places that had completely disappeared because of a terrible war.

"Oh, yes. Everyone died except for Kenneth's mother before I came here. All the cousins, the nieces and nephews, my old mother, everybody gone." Mr. Glibmann looked down silently at his hands. He seemed to be thinking, remembering, and seeing the horror all over again. "I came in 1947 and the whole team moved to Huntsville in 1950. I had worked with

Werner Von Braun in Germany near the end of the war. I was still very young, but I guess I was a little smart because I had an advanced degree when I was twenty in aeronautics." He shrugged his shoulders slightly and took a big breath. "Von Braun got to pick and choose whom he brought to the States. Von Braun had looked for places where the scientists, the German scientists, would be comfortable living, so he chose Huntsville. It's the altitude, you know, the mountains reminded him of a place in Bavaria he loved. And of course, when he came, he brought lots of others and they brought their families and... But my home, I think the Russians made it a big field. Everything, boom!" said Johann. And he threw his hands in the air in a mock explosion. Seeing Gina's shocked face, he reached over and patted her hand and tried for a smile. Johann took another deep breath as he turned away from Gina.

Gina knew about the beginnings of the space program in the US, of Von Braun and the brilliant scientists, he'd brought with him soon after the end of the war. But she'd never actually met anyone that was one of the firsts. She knew about some of the horror stories, as well, but not first hand. How horrific these stories were, and how sad as well. There was no one left of the entire family?

After just a moment, Johann collected himself and turned back to Gina, taking her hand and patting it thoughtfully. "Now it is me and Kenneth, that's it," he said with a shrug of his shoulders. He sat back in his chair and took another deep breath as he wrung his hands together for just a moment. "So, you see, he needs to get married. Oops!" Johann slapped his hand over his mouth as his eyes grew as big as saucers

Gina's eyes narrowed. So that's what this was all about. The old guy needed a niece----in----law and probably lots of great nephews and nieces. Well, she'd have to chew on that one for a while. Soon after Johann had spilled those beans, Gina claimed lesson plans and Colleen to feed and made her escape up the mountain just before the sun set.

Gina watched the cursor blink tirelessly on the monitor screen. Blink, blink, as fast as a heartbeat. Blink, blink. She stared at the screen as Colleen nudged at her leg to go out. With her hand on the

mouse, she pushed the blinking cursor to the send button and clicked. The e----mail was gone. He would either respond or he wouldn't.

"Okay, girl, we'll go out." Gina pulled on a hat, jacket, and mittens and clicked on Colleen's leash before she walked out into the cold night. The air snapped at her nose and she inhaled deeply as the cold air coursed down her like a tall, cold drink.

The weather was bound to break soon. Surely, spring would come. Every night she watched her faithful weatherman on Channel Nineteen give the five----day forecast. Dan the weatherman's forecast said that it might make it up into the fifties next week. If the temperature rebounded that much, it would be a respite from the never----ending cold spell, but still not warm enough to turn off the heater. She would watch the blue flame, the blue flame that snapped and curled and changed into that pair of violet----blue eyes, the violet----blue eyes of…it might be best if she quit thinking about Ken Armstrong for a few days.

------••●●●●••------

Ken logged on to his favorite search engine later that

evening to do a little research on a vector problem he had at work. He'd already made his customary evening to see about Uncle Yo. He decided to check his e----mail first, and as the program ran through its logon, the screen flashed up a sign. He had one message from Star lady. Who on earth was Star lady?

"Dear Ken," it began. Holy mackerel, the woman was e---- mailing him. Ken took a deep breath, and exhaled slowly. He read quickly, feeling his heart slow, and getting his brain under control.

"Dear Ken," he began again. Ken skimmed the letter, and then reread it. So she had deserving students, did she?

He knew how it felt to be a struggling student. Maybe he could get them in for an escorted tour. He knew a guy that worked on the Mars project. Ken closed his eyes and for just a moment, the heart----shaped face and auburn red hair and chocolate brown eyes of Gina Thompson shimmered into view once more. She seemed a rare complete package, brains, personality, and beauty.

Without thinking about his well----thought----out, well---- preserved, survival----from----the---

-fairer----sex skills, he e----mailed back.

"Gina,

I would be delighted to help your students in any way that I can. Why don't we all meet for dinner some night really soon and I can tell them what I can and can't help them with? Have them bring a short outline of the scope of the project. There may be a friend of mine at work that has nearly all the information that they need.

How does the Mexican place on University grab you? They even serve that great Mexican beer.

Ken"

Gina immediately lit the kerosene eater after returning to the house. The temperature had taken yet another dive toward the single digits, so now even the cold little house felt warm to her. She saw her e----mail light flashing and she logged on. Wow, an e----mail from Ken. Gina read and then reread the message. Dinner? Gina's mind flashed through her closet thinking about what she had to wear. Maybe the cleaners got the peanut butter out of her white lamb's wool tunic. Mexican beer, um, delicious. Ken obviously had great taste. But she must and would

58

keep any communiqué between the two of them short and sweet.

"Dear Ken,

I love Mexican beer, especially with lime. I'm sure that my students would be delighted to have dinner to discuss the plans for their very ambitious paper. Did I mention that it's possible for them to earn three credit hours for a two hundred level course if they succeed in my class? I'm sure I did already, and that's why you've agreed to spend an evening with us boring astronomy types. It is very big of you to do this for them. I know they will have some concerns about the paper, so how about if we collaborate?

Maybe the end result will be what Renee and Jimmy canuse."

Gina

PS We'll go Dutch.

"Dear Gina,

I was a student once too. I know how hard and with so little appreciation that they work.

Nix on the Dutch idea. Remember, I am the product

of old world heritage and I wouldn't dream of it. However, your male student may be obliged to pay for his date. I assure you it will build character that will help him through life.

We'll meet on Friday at seven, if that's convenient.

By the way, even though I'm crazy about her, don't bring the dog.

Ken"

"Dear Ken:

I've just talked to my students and Friday has been confirmed. Is 7:00 still good for you?

I'll drive myself and meet you at the front entrance. Gina"

"Dear Gina:

I'll call and see if we need to make a reservation.

This idea to help you students is outstanding. Wish I'd had a teacher like you when I was coming up.

Ken."

Ken sat in his living room reading his e----mail. Reading, but his mind was really stewing about Gina Thompson. He looked around the place he called home, seemingly for the first time, imagining what Gina would think when, and if, she were to see it. His computer sat on a rented table next to a rented chair in his rented apartment. Was his life too impermanent, too ready----made, and too impersonal to interest a woman like Gina? Ken scowled.

He hit the table hard with the flat of his hand, listening to the rattle of loose objects on the tabletop. Things were just getting too out of control and decidedly uncomfortable. What happened to his resolve, his "no women in my life" survival skills? Here he was finding fault with his "you rent to 'em by the week" philosophy, when it had never occurred to him before to even be concerned. And he was going to dinner with her. A real bona fide date.

Unbidden, Gina's heart----shaped face framed with abundant auburn hair floated into his memory. Ken growled in frustration as he grabbed his heavy wool coat and car keys and headed out the door. He wasn't thinking straight. He was usually a level headed, pragmatic kind of person and here he was... He jerked the door open with a muttered curse, dropping his keys onto the top of his foot. He cursed again, something he rarely ever did, as he bent down to pick them up.

"Hey, Ken. Where are you going? You want to come shoot some pool? Some of the guys are meeting down at Groucho's." His across----the----way neighbor had opened his door at the same time as Ken.

"No," Ken growled. "I'm going to go and buy a plant."

****

Gina sat back in her chair reading yet again the e----mail from Ken. "There can't be anything wrong with the man if he likes dogs and has empathy for students," she reasoned.

Excitement from reading Ken's email ratcheted to a giddiness she rarely, if ever, exhibited. Without thinking about her general, albeit momentary, disgust of men, she reached for the phone. She was about to sabotage herself. If she called Janice, that's what she was doing, but something compelled her to pick up the phone. She'd psychoanalyze herself later; right now she was simply too excited.

"Janice, guess what?" Janice was one of Gina's two older sisters. She lived in Athens, Alabama, with her husband, a very sweet and very, very quiet man, and her eight----year----old son, who was a complete monster. Gina felt no compunction to like the kid just because he was her nephew. Jeffy, the monstrous nephew, didn't much like anyone and he showed them his dislike in sometimes explosive, destructive ways—like the time he lit firecrackers under her beach hat (thank goodness she hadn't been wearing it at the time) and blew it to smithereens.

"What?" asked Janice. "I've met a man."

"Oh yeah? What kind of man?"

"He's an engineer and works at Marshall Space Flight Center and he's about six foot four, and he has the neatest eyes and he looks like…well, he looks like…I just know that when I look at him I get a shiver. Maybe it's everything about him."

"Whoa, whoa. Slow down, sis. Now tell me again."

"Well, I went to this little old man's house to buy a kerosene heater he had advertised, and his nephew was there. And the guy, his name is Ken Armstrong, helped me set up the heater and he just e----mailed me and asked me out to dinner and he said that he would help my students and—"

"Whoa, nelly. You're talking about one hundred fifty miles an hour and so far I've gleaned a little out of this story, except that this guy is already Mr. Right."

Mr. Right? Mr. Right? That phrase, that too uncomfortable anxiety----producing phrase, stopped Gina dead in her tracks. Mr. Right? Mr. Right! Hadn't she just been through one long bout of Mr. Wrongs? Okay, okay, it was time to slow down and take stock of this insane plunging on ahead, where angels fear to tread. Gina shook her head and closed her eyes. She breathed deeply and managed to slow her racing heart and, at the same time, her racing mind. With a gargantuan effort, Gina super glued the edges of the wall around her resolve.

"Okay, Janice, maybe you're right. I'll slow down, I know, I won't go. I'll just forget about the whole thing."

"Now wait a minute – just because I told you to slow down doesn't mean that """

"No, you're absolutely right, I'll cancel the dinner."

"Listen. Gina, go to dinner with the guy. Get some help for those students you think so much of, okay? It won't kill you to go. Now, about your social life…I've got just the guy for you."

"Janice!"

"No, listen. He's great. He works in Burt's office, and he's dying to meet you."

"Janice, the last time you got me mixed up with some guy, it was a disaster. He was bald and disgusting. And he was continually trying to 'cop a feel'. How can you be so mean to me?"

Gina closed her eyes and took a deep breath, the headline flashed in her mind:

This just in…Teacher forces big sister to watch old reruns of the "Brady Bunch" in retaliation for unrelenting matchmaking. Details to follow.

Janice's voice intruded on her ever present, ever annoying daydream before she thought up an imagined, but ready at hand, sharp meat cleaver and doing away with her sister once and for all. "He was not bald. He was just a little thin on top and I don't

think he's disgusting. Besides, you can thank me. If I didn't introduce you to all these Mr. Wrongs, how would you know who was Mr. Right?"

"Oh," moaned Gina. "Please don't do me any more favors."

"Somebody's got to get you off that mountain with just the dog for company. You're becoming an absolute hermit." Gina had decided a long while ago that Janice had so little to do, she had a maid once a week for heaven's sake, that she just needed to get her nose into Gina's life. She should concentrate on their other sister, Sally, going through a nasty divorce was the one who could use consolation. Maybe Sally had told her to get lost and not bother her and Janice had finally seen that she meant every word. Gina should practice those words... GET LOST.

"Okay, sometimes dogs are far better company, than creepy men. Who is this Adonis? I guess I could at least get out of doing the dishes for one night."

"Great, I'll fix it all up and call you about the details.

When are you having dinner with this Armstrong guy?"

"On Friday."

"And tell me who his uncle is again?"

"His name is Johann Glibmann and he lives downtown.

Why?"

"I'm just curious who my little sister buys heaters from. I'll call as soon as your other date is set up. Listen to your big sister. I love you, bye."

"Oh, please don't set me up," Gina groaned into the receiver before she fell onto the couch and covered her head with a pillow.

Janice leafed through the Huntsville phone book until she found the name J. Glibmann. The number had a downtown Huntsville exchange that she recognized. She could feel Mr. Glibmann out and see if he would conspire with her to get Gina and Mr. Right together. This Armstrong guy sounded outstanding.

"Hello."

"Mr. Glibmann? I'm Janice, Gina Thompson's big sister. I think she just bought a heater from you?"

"Oh, Gina. What a wonderful young woman. Such great manners, and so funny, and such a lot of brains."

"I'm pleased to hear that from you. So, you like Gina?"

"Oh, very much. She's such a wonderful girl. She came over today and we just chatted, just to get acquainted."

"Wonderful, that's wonderful. So this is why I'm calling... our family wants very much for Gina to have some sort of a social life. We're all worried that she spends too much time on the mountain with just a dog for company."

"I know just how you feel. That nephew of mine, oh my. He's always with the computer and never with people. I worry for him, too."

"Mr. Glibmann, I'll be blunt. Since we seem to have the same concerns, how about if we collaborate? Maybe the end result will be what all of us want. I'm afraid the fact is if we don't do something to hurry this along, well, if they are destined to be together, then maybe we can push destiny a little. If we wait for Gina to make a first move, I just know I'll be eighty before she ever settles down."

Mr. Glibmann chuckled into the phone. "Well, darling, we'll just see what we can do. Why don't you call me next week and we'll discuss some more moves. Now, auf wiedersen. I'll call you soon."

Chapter Four

Gina anxiously stood in the entryway of El Camino Real, the Mexican bistro, at the appointed time on Friday night. Her students sat on a nearby bench with their heads together, discussing the outline of their project. Gina glanced at her watch----7: 04 p.m.

She looked about the restaurant, appreciatively admiring the many piñatas, the murals, the music, and the scurrying and handsome Hispanic waiters. A mural of a mythical Mayan paradise in vibrant blues and deep reds was painted behind the wall of the cashier station.

The place smelled wonderful. Soft Latin love songs floated out of the sound system. Despite her ambivalence about being on a date, she was glad she was there. Especially since her stomach was rumbling with hunger that vied with her fluttering nerves. She inhaled deeply of the enchanting aromas just as a blast of cold air came barreling through the door.

Gina turned and in stepped Ken. Her heart definitely beat a little faster at the sight of him. He looked so handsome with the cold burnishing his cheeks. He'd gotten his hair cut. He wore a classy navy blue sweater and gray slacks. He looked like a model on the cover of a men's fashion magazine and he seemed to be completely oblivious of the fact that he was gorgeous.

She felt shivers travel up her spine, fireworks went off, and a 150----piece Sousa band played loudly in her head. Gina smiled and extended her trembling hand. And then something happened that she'd instinctively known happened rarely. Ken smiled.

"This place is wonderful. I haven't been here in so long. I'd forgotten how terrific it is," Gina said with a smile.

Gina wore a long, white, fuzzy sweater and white slacks and the sight of her absolutely took his breath away. When she looked at him, her eyes shone so

71

brightly they sent a personal message straight to his heart. The subtle beating pulse under his ear tapped slowly and then quickened as she smiled at him again. Warmth coiled inside his chest, tugging at his heartstrings. He hadn't felt anything like this in a long time. It was going to be a very pleasant evening.

Ken placed his hand on Gina's back to lead her across the room to their booth when the host ushered them to their table. Ken felt the pull of desire shoot through him when he touched her. Reluctantly, he let go of Gina's waist and shoved into the seat next to her. He moved a little and subtly made sure his leg touched hers a tiny bit. He was so aware of Gina as he sat just a few inches away. He smiled and chatted with Jimmy and Renee and put his subtle awareness of Gina on hold. He held out his hand for the folder Jimmy and Renee had brought with them and began leafing through it.

"Renee, tell me all about your project," said Ken. He read through the bulleted points quickly while Renee summarized their project. It was an impressive-- -looking outline, very professional. Ken read with one eye on the paper and listened with one ear. Gina's presence took up the rest of his attention.

For a moment, Ken forgot where he was. He was so engrossed listening to Renee and Jimmy that he forgot he was talking to two teenagers about their project. He was having the best time he'd had in a long, long while, because he was also with their teacher.

Gina spoke about her students with animation, and she was eager and enthusiastic. Ken realized she was the furthest thing from self----involved of any woman he had ever been around and somehow that surprised him a great deal. He noticed her nose turned pink right at the tip every once in a while. Maybe she was blushing. Perhaps she'd learned to school her emotions enough to keep a full----faced blush under control. Ken thought he would like to make her blush just to see where the pink on the end of her nose would spread to other parts of her anatomy.

He couldn't remember when he had smiled so much. The food was great, the beer delicious, and the company? Ken's thoughts came to a grinding halt. That sore spot on his heart wasn't healed over, not by a long shot.

Gina was glad she'd asked Ken, for her students' sakes, if not for hers. She watched Ken speak animatedly with Renee and Jimmy as his ruddy, masculine face lit up. Every once in a while he turned to her to ask a question and then he'd smile. Those smiles warmed her from the top to the bottom and made her feel like she'd just sipped a little glass of whiskey.

When he turned and looked at her, his expression was full of warmth and good humor and little laugh lines crinkled at the corners of his eyes. Her insides turned into a million butterflies, all clamoring at the same time for attention. She closed her eyes and inwardly, she sighed. She could hear her big sister, Janice, hands on hips, leaning over to give her a lecture: "Now, you give the guy a chance. Don't let this 'could be the one' man slip away, just because you're stubborn." She mentally switched her brain to the 'off' position and tried to pick up on what she'd missed of the conversation.

"So Ken," she said, and then stopped. She cleared her throat. The task at hand was to help her students earn those three hours of applied science, not to satisfy her libido. "So Ken," she continued. "When do you think we could bother you at work? I've got plenty of personal time built up and I can just call their parents and make arrangements. If we go through the school, it gets pretty bureaucratic with paperwork. If you'll just give me your work number, I'll be able to relay that to Jimmy and Renee's parents, and it should be sufficient as a contact number. Would that be okay, to come to Marshall, I mean? "

"Sure. Why don't you all come about ten o'clock on Wednesday, and then we could go to lunch at that little German place on Redstone Arsenal?."

Gina thought she had died and gone to heaven. There was even a lunch invitation? It was too much to wrap her head around.

Abruptly, the expression on Ken's face changed. It was as though someone had turned the light off. Gina had a lunch invitation from a man who looked like he'd like to take it back.

"Well, if you're sure we won't be too much trouble?"

"I'll have to e----mail you about that, okay?" Ken said, ducking his head down.

An undercurrent of something vibrated around the

table. He'd been so open, so warm, and now, Gina thought, well, if something is too good to be true, it usually is.

This is just too put together, too perfect, Ken thought. So perfect it can't be for real. I'm not waiting around to see if it is. I'll call myself chicken later.

"Maybe you guys should head out of here," Gina said. "I'll see for myself just fine, thanks.

Good grief, she'd put her foot in it, and said too much, let too much slip. After all, she was a twin, and life might never be easy if she fended for herself or had just herself for company, having been with someone else since the spark of conception. Being alone was okay — and she was getting used to it. Maybe she'd turn out to be an old maid school teacher. Jimmy cleared his throat loudly.

"Well, Ms. Thompson, we'll see you on Monday, and Mr.Armstrong, we'll see you on Wednesday." "Call me Ken, and that'll be just fine."

Gina made a quick attempt at finishing her beer after her two students left the restaurant. Ken's scrutiny, as well as the curl of warmth that seemed never to leave her tummy when he was near, had her feeling quite out of control. She dragged on her coat and felt her lips twitch in lieu of a smile. She got up quickly and they walked toward the front of the restaurant.

She wanted to reach out and touch him to see if she imagined this feeling, this curl of warmth like the beginning of a fire burning in her. Was it Ken's presence, or was it just the enchiladas? She watched his finely molded hands as he paid the bill and wondered what they would feel like if he touched her. She watched his wide, deep chest as he shrugged into his jacket. Her eyes moved upward again and gazed at his strong chin, lightly dusted with stubble, and his rugged face. She felt the warmth inside her continue to spread like fingers to every part of her body. Catching her breath and her runaway, out of control mind, she turned and looked back into the restaurant to stop her thoughts. With a grumble, she turned away and headed toward the door. Girlish romances were not her style and she wasn't about to start now. Hadn't she just been through it with the creepy, lecher of the century? Gina glanced over her shoulder at Ken. She could just see the headlines:

This just in… Teacher from Grissom High arrested for jumping on innocent men in Mexican restaurant… Film at 11.

She shook her head to dispel the thought along with her resident TV reporter. That insistent reporter that lived inside her head no matter how many times she'd tried to give him the boot. She'd have to take it slow. She'd make herself take this very slowly.

Besides, she really didn't know if the man was even interested.

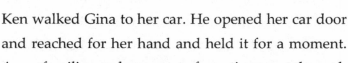

Ken walked Gina to her car. He opened her car door and reached for her hand and held it for a moment. An unfamiliar undercurrent of emotion went through him. He could not stop the smile that spread over his face. "I'm looking forward to seeing you and your students in a few days."

"That's great. They are so thrilled, and so am I."

Ken saw the end of Gina's nose turn so brightly pink that he could see it in the harsh glare of the parking lot lights. A flush spread from her cheeks all the way to her hairline.

Ken's smile became an encompassing grin. He'd made her blush. This was fun. Forget worrying about not getting involved for now. He reached over, and bracing his hands on each of her shoulders, leaned down, and gave her a kiss. Her lips were warm and soft, and pulses of electricity shot through him. His head reeled. She felt so good. She smelled like lavender and some light lemon fragrance and a very Gina scent. His hands wandered up and down Gina's back, pulling her even closer, feeling the urgency deepen. He lost himself in that kiss, feeling the warmth radiate from inside her jacket, the softness of her face so close to his, until a tiny moan escaped from both of them at precisely the same moment. Ken pulled away first, looked down at her, and smiled. He wished they were anywhere but in the parking lot of a restaurant.

Gina said nothing, but put her hand up to stroke his cheek very briefly. She turned away and got into her car. Before she closed the door, she looked up at him, smiled, and gave a wave.

Ken lifted his hand as Gina pulled out of the parking lot. He watched until the red spots of her taillights faded into the night.

The following Wednesday, Gina, Jimmy, and Renee met at the main entrance of the research, development, and engineering building in a large complex of buildings that was the Marshall Space Flight Center. The structures were imposing, rising many stories out of a wooded area off one of the main highway interchanges in Huntsville.

Ken met them in the lobby and signed them in. He shook Jimmy's and Renee's hands and opened the door with his key card and ushered them through a long corridor to a bank of cubicles.

Since the past Saturday night, Ken had built his safety wall around him again, his emotional safeguard. He would not ride this all----consuming tide of emotion that permeated his mind night and day since he'd seen Gina last. He was going to be Mr. Unapproachable, Mr. Nonchalant, Mr. Whatever. Because being emotionally involved with anyone was no longer an option for him. He stood back and watched Gina and her students take in the atmosphere. The three of them were beaming and grinning like kids on Christmas morning.

"Wow, this is too cool," said Jimmy, for about the fourth time.

Ken led them through a glassed in gangway that looked down into an experimental area. The gigantic room housed simulators that looked like sawed----off spacecraft. Men poked about between the huge pieces of equipment, jotting quickly on clipboards, and shouting above the noise of the engines and equipment.

Ken watched Gina's brightened face, soaking in the atmosphere around her like a big sponge. She was like an excited little girl. He couldn't help himself: he reached out, took her hand, and squeezed. She really was the most incredible woman. She'd worn this forest----green business suit that made her skin look like honey. Her eyes were shining like stars, and he couldn't help but wish that maybe it was being with him as well as being at Marshall that made them shine so.

"I'll tell you what," Jimmy said, trying to get his teacher's attention, even though she seemed quite preoccupied at the moment. "How about if we eat here, you know, soak up some atmosphere?"

"That's not a bad idea," Ken said. "They usually make a pretty good lasagna on Wednesdays, but first, let's see my buddy about some stats on your project."

Ken led them down the stairs into a huge room that was divided into cubicles with no windows and row upon row of glaring fluorescent lights. Each of the room dividers was padded, and the sides were carpeted. Not that the noise could be completely tuned out like it would be in a regular office that had doors. Gina supposed it cut down on some of the racket, except, as now, when the occasional engineer stuck his head out into the hall and shouted, "Anybody ordering out for lunch?"

Ken made his way down the labyrinth to his cubicle. Gina looked around with frank curiosity. The man was as neat as a pin and obviously would not have the neat and tidy police visiting him anytime soon. His papers were all stacked up, corners matching, his pens and pencils were in a little cup holder, even his coffee cup was centered on a coaster, and his sticky notes had their own neat little container.

Ken introduced Gina and the kids to his colleague Jeff Goldberg. Mr. Goldberg began his planned talk for the students as he'd had a heads up from Ken about Jimmy and Renee's project. His words trailed off into silence when Gina's smile caught his attention. Jeff's jaw hung open and he couldn't keep his eyes off Gina. Ken cleared his throat roughly.

"We'll just go get a cup of coffee while you educate the kids." Ken held Gina's elbow as he led her to the kitchen area.

"This room is so massive, I'd get lost and starve to death before someone could find me," said Gina as she sat at the round table in the kitchenette. Ken pulled two mugs from the cabinet and poured out coffee for each of them.

"Ah, no you wouldn't. I'd make sure you at least found the coffee pot."

They sat together at the table and sipped their coffee, but the silence between them became decidedly uncomfortable. One woman in a short sleeved, over large, flowered dress came into the break room. She certainly made a splash. If she wanted to be noticed there would be no way she couldn't stand out with her head of frizzy shoulder----length red hair and bright clothes.

"Well, hello, Ken," said the woman. She stared at Gina and Gina, taken by surprise by the scrutiny, stared back. The woman looked down to read the guest badge dangling from the collar of Gina's dark green, conservative suit. The woman's frizzy red hair had been teased so that the sides of her head seemed to be almost parallel with her shoulders. Gina, and looked down at the edge of her coffee cup, doing her best not to stare at the woman's outlandish hair or feel uncomfotable from the woman's staring.

"Hi, Myrna, this is Gina Thompson. She and a few of her high school students are here for a tour," said Ken as he gestured to Gina.

"Glad to meet you." The woman smiled at Gina and a little of the tension she'd brought into the tiny kitchen dissipated. Before Gina could get a word in with Myrna, Jeff brought Renee and Jimmy into the kitchen.

"This is really neat, Mr. Armstrong. We've got all kinds of great information," said Jimmy animatedly as he came into the room. The high schooler's shinning faces and body language said it all.

"That's terrific, Jimmy. Now let's go downstairs for

lunch." Ken looked pointedly at Jeff, making sure he knew that he wasn't invited. Jeff got the message loud and clear. He shook Gina's hand and waved to the kids and then left.

The foursome made their way down into the basement to the huge building's cafeteria. The cafeteria was a hubbub of movement, sounds, and smells.

"Oh. No lasagna today. Oh, well, the tacos are good," said Ken as he consulted the blackboard menu that hung from the wall.

"Yeah, that sounds good."

They each took tacos from the steam trays, loaded their plates with the fixings and drinks, and found a table in the crowded room. There were all types sitting around in the huge room, and Gina stared openly. There were a few men in white shirts and dark trousers with pencil protectors in their front pockets. And a few fellows in t----shirts with scarves draped dramatically around their necks, some hanging down past their jean----clad knees.

Many of the women were in dresses and skirts, while some obviously didn't care what they looked like and sported sweat shirts and jeans.

Ken watched Gina's expression as she surveyed the room. "Yeah, it's dork city around here."

Gina looked up knowing that she'd been caught staring. Slightly embarrassed, she adjusted her gaze to the top of her plate and giggled.

The foursome ate in silence for just a few seconds when a loud crash focused their attention to the cash register area.

"What do you mean, there's no lasagna?" exclaimed a man standing with his legs braced apart, glowering at the cashier. He was a squat little fellow, bald with black thick----rimmed glasses. His face was red with anger and he clutched the cafeteria tray to his chest as though the flimsy thing was holding him up.

"I'm sorry, sir," the young cashier said anxiously. "We couldn't get the noodles from the supplier today, so we had to make extra tacos instead."

"This is absolutely ridiculous. I always eat lasagna on Wednesday and today will be absolutely no exception."

"But sir, we have none made."

"Well, you just make some right now."

Gina stared blatantly at the entire exchange. The enraged customer acted like he had lost touch with reality. And perhaps his head was so far in to rockets and the stars, that he had most certainly lost his fragile grip on the here and now.

The scene embarrassed Ken, although there was no reason why it should. "Uh, sorry about that."

The squat little man at the cash register threw the tray toward the kitchen, and stalked out of the door. The entire cafeteria took a collective sigh of relief before dissolving into nervous giggles.

Gina turned back to Ken with a smile, and saw the crease of worry in his brow. "Don't worry about it. They should've handed him a can of lasagna. The canned lasagna with the curly noodles is pretty good," she said with a smile.

Ken burst out laughing, Renee giggled, and Jimmy, who had ignored the whole exchange in favor of his tacos, looked up in surprise.

"Did I miss something?"

Renee patted Jimmy on the arm as everyone went back to their lunch.

Gina looked up and did a double take when she saw a woman in a black jersey dress. The dress clung to every part of her as she slinked, not walked, over to their table. And did she slink. She stared rudely in turn at Gina, Jimmy, and Renee for a second and then turned her attention to Ken. She stroked her crimson fingernails against the back of his neck. Ken jerked back and then looked like he had turned to stone. He did not look at the woman in black, but concentrated on his iced tea. For a moment, Gina felt an uncontrollable wave of jealousy. Who in the name of Copernicus was this? This slinky, snarky condescending woman acted like she owned Ken.

"Oh, Ken, honey. Why haven't you called?" crooned the woman. Her voice oozed with saccharine as she spoke and as she looked at Gina.

Ken's face went red with embarrassment as he looked up at the woman. "Rachel, I wasn't supposed to call you," he said gruffly.

"Oh, Kenny, why can't we let bygones be bygones," said the woman as she practically draped herself into Ken's lap. Honest, she sat right in his lap. Gina squelched the urge to say, 'get a room.'

Ken squirmed and roughly shoved the woman off his lap and back up into a standing position. He desperately wanted Gina to know that this woman was not his girlfriend, especially since his feelings about Gina leaned toward the emotional and not the intellectual kind. He cleared his throat; if he had to be rude, he guessed he'd just have to.

"These are my friends, Gina Thompson, Jimmy and Renee," he said, gesturing around the table and keeping his eyes on Gina while completely avoiding eye contact with the other woman. "They've come for a tour today." Ken continued to remain polite, although it would feel terrific if he could stand up and yell at Rachel. He did not want to cause a scene. He kept his eyes on Gina's expression, did not look at Rachel, and smiled so hard he thought his face might just crack. Gina's head stayed ducked down and thankfully missed of Rachel's scowl to the top of Gina's head.

"Oh really?" Rachel stroked her fingernails up the back of Ken's neck in an attempt to gain his attention. Ken shook off her hand like he was swatting at an annoying insect and still would not look at her. The woman sniffed, turned on her heel, and left slinking across the floor.

Jimmy had been concentrating with all the usual teenage boy's focus on his tacos during the entire exchange. He looked up just as the woman began her oily glide across the room. "Look at her legs, Oops, sorry. I know that's not polite, but she's got scrawny legs, just like a chicken," he said soto voce.

Ken started; looked around quickly at Rachel, went red and then white trying to take in a big gulp of air as he choked on a mouthful of food. Gina jumped up, and her plated taco did a graceful flip, coming down oh so slowly, and landing squarely in Renee's lap. Renee sprang up from her chair, lost her balance, and over compensating, her upper body sprawled onto the table. Jimmy jumped up and knocked his chair over backwards grabbing for Renee to steady her. His hand caught the edge of his tray. The tray launched itself into a perfect somersault before it hit the floor with a huge crash, splattering milk, taco meat, and chocolate pudding all over the floor and tabletop. Gina gasped, turned red, and at turns, pounded Ken on the back and pulled his arms above his head. Jimmy's voice rose above the chaos, "Do you want me to get him a glass of water?"

"Are you all right, are you all right?" Gina asked over and Over again.

Ken waved his hand to ward off his three guests, while the entire cafeteria, patrons and workers alike, stopped in tableau and simply stared.

He finally caught his breath and sat back in his chair. Everyone around them slowly returned to normal.

"It's just too funny," he said, looking up into Gina's face. He stopped and then shook his head for just a moment and then laughed shaking his head. "That's exactly what Uncle Yo says about her legs."

Gina just rolled her eyes as she slumped back down in her chair, trying to avoid the big blob of chocolate pudding near her foot.

"Okay, you two, let's get this cleaned up!" Gina, Jimmy, and Renee took an entire container of napkins to mop up taco meat and milk off their clothes and the cafeteria staff mopped up the mess on the floor. Slowly, the rest of the cafeteria returned to normal. "Wow," said Gina as she slumped back into her chair. "I think I've had about enough excitement for one day. I think I'll go back to high school where it's quieter."

•••●●●••

The temperature warmed up to thirty----eight degrees later that evening and Gina decided to take an extra----long walk with Colleen. The exercise would do her good, and maybe she could clear out a few cobwebs lingering in her mind. After looking at all the chubby computer potatoes at NASA, she decided to make a renewed effort to get in at least a few miles each day with Colleen. And she'd just have to talk to herself about Ken Armstrong during her walk. She went over all the pros and cons of their rather tentative relationship. Was he a Mr. Right or the Mr. Right? He certainly seemed wonderful, dashing, smart, loyal, caring…

"Man, Gina, he's starting to sound like you think he's the poster boy for the Boy Scouts of America," she muttered to herself.

And physically…Gina stopped her mind right there. She could not be held responsible if she thought about those big blue eyes and that wonderfully broad chest.

Did she have enough stamina to deal with another man? What if he turned out to be a louse like all of the others? Most of her time and energy was spent on school. It was more than a full---- time job with all of the prep time at home, in the library, and at the planetarium. Would any man put up with her staying up till all hours with astronomical data charts? Gina's breath came out in a big puff and collided with the chilled air. She stood on a little overlook on the side of the road and stared at the bright lights of Huntsville far below. It looked like a fairyland, the

lights twinkling and sparkling against the blue---
-black sky. Yeah, a fairyland. It was just too bad that
she couldn't figure out who her Prince Charming
really was.

Things were so simple in the old days. You were
locked up in a castle by some nasty old troll, your
golden hair stuck out the casement window and
fluttered in the breeze like a banner for help. Then
Prince Charming would come dashing in on his white
charger, cut the troll to ribbons (uck), and gallop off
into the sunset with you on the front of his saddle. Of
course, damsels never mentioned all the bruises they
got from being bounced around on the pommel of a
saddle. Or, saints preserve us, how bad poor old
Prince Charming smelled because he'd been in a
sweaty suit of armor for days looking for you, without
a motel, hotel, or hostel in sight.

But when Gina forced her eyes out of focus on the
panoramic scene that spilled out in front of her, she
could actually see him, her Prince Ken—er—
Charming. He rode a huge black horse. The horse
wore a flounce around his Saddle blanket that
fluttered around as it pranced and an elaborate boot
on each hoof. When he took off his helmet, his hair

stuck out every which way that was too endearing, and he smiled at her with those violet----blue eyes.

Gina shook her head rather sharply. She pulled on Colleen's lead and headed back to the house.

"You know you could have nudged me or something," she said to Colleen. "I mean, here I was imagining some crazy scene with Ken as the knight in shining armor, and what you do? I made a fool of myself in front of me, for heaven's sake. I embarrassed myself, and you just sat there and looked at the glittering lights of the city. I act as though there is absolutely nothing in my head at all. And there isn't with the way I'm carrying on. If I don't cut the daydreaming out, I won't be able to live with myself. All my brains will be used up on childish notions. Oh, Gina, cool it. If it's going to happen, it's going to happen, and no trolls are around to lock you up in some castle. Besides, you can't get Ken inside the castle unless you know his special knightly phone number."

After Gina and Colleen returned to the house, they sat together in front of the kerosene heater, absorbing the warmth and camaraderie of one another. Gina tried not to think about Ken but images of his handsome face intruded continually. It was time for her pragmatic self to come out of hiding. Someone had to help her with this dilemma, and by default, it might as well be her. She sighed as she snuggled deeper into her quilt and imagined Ken's arms around her.

Wow, what a man.

———————•●●●●●●•———————

Chapter Five

"Janice, I just don't think it's a good idea. For heaven's sake, Gina has her master's degree, and she's thirty years old. Don't you think she can pick her own men without help from us? Why don't you just go bother Sally?"

"No, I do not, Andy. And Sally has basically told me she'd kill me if I spoke to her about men again. She's still getting over her divorce.

"But, don't you remember the story about the married band director? Old Mrs, now what is her name— you know Mom's friend from the Rotary Club, was only too happy to spill the beans about him and Gina to Mom. Gina decidedly needs our help. Now, 'O brother of the womb,' get over there and check this Armstrong guy out and report back to me. His address is 550 Executive Drive, Apartment 204. I think he'll be great, but I only have second hand information."

"All right, all right, big sister. Your wish is my command. I'll go over with a six pack and check him out," said Andy as he sketched a salute over the phone to Janice.

"Andy..."

"Yes, I'm going, I'm going, right now."

Andy drove to the address Janice had given him and was pleased that he had managed to arrive by 5:20 p.m. Even Janice would be happy about that. And, oh yes, the game would be on at 6:00 p.m., and he'd be able to find out lots about Ken while watching with him.

The apartment complex was nice enough. It wasn't terribly classy, but it had a pool and a landscaped area with a hiking trail around the perimeter. Ken's place was really close to his own apartment and somewhere in the back of his mind that pleased Andy.

Ken answered the door, dressed in a t----shirt and jeans, and looked a little startled to see Andy on his doorstep.

"Hey, how you doing? I told you I'd return the favor someday for helping my sister," said Andy as he leaned in past the door jam, looking around quizzically at Ken's place. "Have you eaten?"

"No, I—"

"Well, no problem then. I've ordered a pizza for us. Hope you don't like anchovies. Now tell me how the infamous meeting with the brilliant students went on Wednesday?"

Andy pushed past him into the room. Ken was too startled to say anything, and felt his jaw slide south as he watched Andy deposit the beer in the fridge as he continued to talk.

He snapped his mouth shut with some effort and watched Andy bustle around in his refrigerator as he talked to him a mile a minute. But Ken appreciatively noticed the six pack of dark brown ale Andy deposited in his refrigerator. Good stuff. Andy finished putting away the beer and stood next to him pounding him on the back with brotherly camaraderie.

"Hey, we can watch the game," said Andy standing in from of the TV, messing with the remote until he found the appropriate channel.

"Game?" Ken said weakly.

"Yeah, man, Auburn versus Tennessee. Don't you follow basketball?"

"Well, not too much. I—"

"Hey with your height, I'm surprised that they didn't recruit you in high school."

"Well, I actually wrestled and played tennis," said Ken. Until that moment it had not occurred to him that tennis and wrestling were individual sports, no teamwork, just doing it on your own. He wondered, briefly, if that said something strange and off----center about his personality.

"You wrestled? Cool. What weight class?"

"Uh, 165. I was so tall I really had an unfair advantage sometimes, and then other times, the little stocky guys clobbered me," said Ken. It was easy to warm up to Andy with his incessant but friendly chatter. The man was so open. Ken decided right there that he liked Andy a lot.

Andy gave a short bark of a laugh. "I would have

liked seeing you get clobbered by a little guy like me. Ah, sweet revenge."

Ken laughed. "Yeah, I would've liked to see you get a charge out of it, too."

"Okay, Janice, I checked the guy out. He likes pepperoni on his pizza, dark brown ale, and wrestling, Greco----Roman type. As far as I can tell, he's very cool, very bright, wipes his mouth at the appropriate time, and doesn't belch just because he's in the company of other men," reported Andy. He and Ken had watched the game, and talked the whole time about important and not so important things. It didn't take past the first quarter for Andy to decide that he really liked him.

"Good grief, send a child on a man's errand..."

"What do you mean? He's a great guy. I really mean it. I don't think he will ever mess with Gina's head and he's a gentleman, okay? So, stop worrying. I told you she's a big girl."

"Did you check out the bathroom and make sure there were no women's cosmetics, or the closet to see if his girlfriend had left any clothes there? We want to make sure that this guy is for real. What if he is fooling around with someone else? Men, sometimes y'all aren't worth well, anyway…. Argh!" Janice hollered loud enough to be heard all the way from Athens, thirty miles away.

"Now, I have just the girl for you."

"Listen, Uncle Yo…"

Ken sat across from his uncle in Johann's little kitchen, having a cup of coffee.

"Nah, nah, I have arranged everything," said Johann with a wave of his hand. "The maître de at Michael's has my credit card, I paid for it, and the girl will meet you at the restaurant."

"But, Uncle Yo—"

"You have to go. I've already talked to her grandma," Johann said. He waved his finger under Ken's nose as though he was a little boy. He gave him that look. That Uncle Johann look that said, "No arguments will be tolerated."

"She's twenty----five and very nice. I think she teaches kindergarten. Now you have to go. I will have the egg on my face if you don't. Friday night, 7:00 p.m., at Michael's. I see you!" said Johann as he handed Ken his jacket, and ushered him to the door. He pushed Ken's back through the door, and as Ken turned around and opened his mouth to speak, Johann stopped him with a gesture. "Oh, her name is Susan. Susan Chambers. Tus!" he said as he closed the door soundly, but gently in Ken's face.

Johann picked up the kitchen phone after he heard Ken's jeep pull out of the drive. He dialed a number in Athens, Alabama.

"Hello?"

"Hello, Janice? This is Johann Glibmann." "Oh, hi. So, how is our project coming along?" "Well, I have news my dear..."

----●•●●•-

"I can't believe Uncle Johann would set me up like this. He must be either senile or completely desperate," said Ken after he reached his apartment.

Ken remembered the Chambers family, vaguely.

They had been friends of his parents. Somehow the face of the girl that would have been seven years his junior could not be summoned to memory.

Ken growled as he dragged himself into the center of the floor in his living room. He shoved his hands in his pockets, made one complete turn around the room, scowling. Since he'd met Gina, for some reason that he could not fathom himself, he'd taken all the old newspapers that he used in his research, a stack about three feet high that had sat under his window, to the recycling. He'd taken down the curtains over the one window, washed them, and used a glass cleaner on all the corners of the windowsill. He'd rearranged the furniture for more of what he'd thought was a homey atmosphere, more Feng Shui. He'd even gone to the local do----it---- yourself big box store and bought a rubber tree and a plant that was kind of a green something to sit on the now polished coffee table.

But, no matter what he did to the place, it still looked rented and impermanent. He wondered what Gina would think of a place like this. He scowled again. Why did he care what Gina thought of his place? It wasn't like he planned to live here forever. Maybe he'd buy a house next year and shelter some of that money he was pulling in from Uncle Sam.

No, to be completely honest, he'd probably just buy another computer. Ken slumped on the couch. A heart----shaped face framed by luxuriant auburn hair and a pair of deep brown eyes floated before his mind's eye. There was just no way around it. When he thought of her, he smiled, and that was something he rarely did. She made his heart beat a little faster, and he just wanted her, wanted her in every way imaginable.

Ken heaved a big sigh, and furrowed his brow. Uncle Yo had hooked him up with some bimbo. Well, she could, he supposed, be a nice woman. Gross. He supposed he'd have to save the family's face and go to Michael's on Friday night.

Butch sauntered up to the couch and watched Ken for a few seconds. The cat, without ceremony, jumped agilely onto Ken's lap and rubbed up against his hand for attention.

"You know the nice thing about you, Butch? You don't drool like that dog of Gina's. Dogs drool, cats rule. But, then again, you don't come when you're called either. That is the basic difference between a dog and a cat. You're either so smart that you refuse to be trained or you're so dumb you can't be trained. Well, which is it, Butch? Are you smarter than Colleen?" The rumble from Butch's purring vibrated Ken's lap and sent his thoughts down the seldom----traveled path of witticism and incredulity.

"'The Difference Between a Dog and a Cat' by Ken Armstrong, beer connoisseur extraordinairé

"A cat is furry, so is a dog. But Gina isn't. Dogs and cats come in a variety of colors; some shed, and many leave their hair where it isn't wanted. Gina on the other hand doesn't shed, but she did leave a few of those lovely auburn hairs on my jacket."

He'd looked at those bits of Gina long and hard before he had gently let them fall from his fingers into the trash.

"Now, back to this earth----shatteringly deep essay. A dog can be trained to come when it is called, and even help blind and crippled people." He wondered if Gina might be amiable like one of those golden retrievers that could be trained to recognize the wheat bread as opposed to the rye bread for their quadriplegic masters. Would Gina bring him some pumpernickel if he asked for it? He'd certainly get her some.

Lord, what was he doing?

"Ken, you are in deep stuff if all you can think about is this gorgeous woman even when you're trying to make up a silly essay about the difference between cats and dogs." He sighed deeply; time to get back to normal, whatever that was. "It is time to cut out the schlock and get on with it. No more women!"

Ken dumped Butch on the floor, grabbed his coat and bag, and headed out to the gym. Maybe a few hours of lifting weights would cool his heels.

Gina wandered through the aisles at the local big box discount store just browsing around. She usually didn't frequent this store because she always found something she knew she just couldn't live without. It was hard to save money and come to a place like this because the deals were always so great. So, who could pass them up?

The store excursion was really an excuse to get out of the house. Whenever she looked at the computer all she could think about was Ken. She decided she could get more done if she didn't think about him. Midterms were coming up, and she still had to create her astronomy class exam.

As Gina cruised down the pet care aisle looking intently at the dog section, her cart collided with a man that was perusing the cat section.

"I'm sorry, did I—?"

Gina stopped and sucked in her breath. The man standing in front of her with his big toe wedged under the wheel of her cart was Ken Armstrong. He looked bedraggled, irritated. He had on a pair of very used gray sweats and his hair was wet and plastered down.

"Ken! Oh Holy Moly, is your toe, okay?"

Ken calmly looked down and gently rubbed his toe through his shoe with his other foot. "Yeah, I think you mostly got the shoe."

"I'm really sorry. What are you doing here anyway? Do you have a cat? I didn't know you had a cat." Gina promptly shut her mouth as she felt the blood rush to her cheeks.

Ken chuckled. "Yes, his name is Butch. He's the inside

kind of cat. I'm afraid he's getting to be as big as a cartoon cat. Are you here buying stuff for Colleen?"

"Well, really I'm just kind of here. The trouble with this store is I'll always see something I can use and end up spending money." Gina looked at her card, willing the blood to go somewhere besides her cheeks and nose. She looked up and smiled. After all, she was just really glad to see him. "You didn't tell me you had a cat. My regard for you has climbed another ten points," Gina teased. "See," she tried to explain. "If someone has a pet, then they are responsible for them, and they have to care for and nurture them."

"Yeah, but there are plenty of people who don't."

"I know, but I think you are in the category that does. So tell me about your cat."

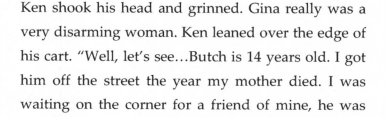

Ken shook his head and grinned. Gina really was a very disarming woman. Ken leaned over the edge of his cart. "Well, let's see…Butch is 14 years old. I got him off the street the year my mother died. I was waiting on the corner for a friend of mine, he was coming over on his bike, when a tiny kitten ran across the street and jumped on me. Of course, I had to carry him home and ask my mother if I could keep him. I remember it like it was yesterday. She stood there with her hands on her hips shaking her head. Being a fastidious housekeeper, we never had any pets, too hard and too time consuming to clean up after. But she relinquished."

This is great. That's the most information I've ever gotten out of the man. And here he is talking a million miles an hour about his cat.

"When can I see this wondrously spectacular feline?" Gina teased.

"You can come right now if you like. I know, I'll buy stuff for nachos, that's easy and I have beer at the house."

Gina looked at her watch. "6:30 p.m. already, no wonder I'm starved. All right, you're on. I can't stay too long; Colleen will wonder where I am. You know us nurturing types—we have to be attentive to our responsibilities."

Gina pushed her empty cart back to the front while

Ken paid for his purchases and then followed Gina to her car.

Gina laughed as she stuck her head out the car window and called. "Now I can go woo your cat and make him love me the way Colleen loves you." Gina clamped her mouth shut. That was just a little too close to the real truth.

What are you doing, Thompson? Oh Gina, didn't you promise yourself that you weren't going to get involved again until later, when things in your life calmed down? At the rate I'm going, I may be ninety before that happens.

Ken laughed as he got into his jeep and pulled out of the parking lot with Gina following. She muttered to herself the first three miles of the trip and then put the brakes on her brain. "Enough is enough. Just go have some fun for a change." She cranked the radio up and listened to a very loud rendition of Mozart's "Eine Kleine Nacht Musik" to drown out her thoughts.

•••●●●•••

Gina looked around with abject curiosity at the combo kitchen, office area as Ken showed her into his

111

apartment a few minutes later. It was a nice place for being just an apartment, and Gina had seen tons of them as well as lived in a few.

Ken looked over the top of the refrigerator door, "Would you like a beer? Take your coat off and turn on the TV if you want to."

"Okay, a beer sounds great," said Gina as she shrugged out of her parka and laid it across the arm of the sofa. "Now, where's the infamous Butch?"

"If you're brave," said Ken's voice floating from the kitchen, "you can look under the bed. I can't guarantee what you'll find besides Butch."

The man was exaggerating. She'd never seen a cleaner person, man or woman. Everything, everything was neat and tidy.

She was sure that she'd never have to clean Ken's bathroom. Maybe he should come over and clean hers. Gina walked down the short hall past a spare room and a bath into the bedroom. She found a light switch through the grope----and----feel method. Ken had a king----sized bed, which he probably needed, and a matching night stand and dresser. As Gina looked around her gaze settled on a painting over the dresser. She knew she shouldn't, but she walked over to get a closer look. By Copernicus, it was a painting of a knight in a burnished black suit of armor. A golden eagle with outstretched wings dominated the armor breastplate and the knight held his helm under his arm, as he sat confidently on the huge black war horse. The knight in the picture had long shaggy hair, violet----blue eyes, and pronounced cheekbones. Gina swallowed hard, hoping her heart would lodge itself back into her chest. The painting was so close to the imagined knight in her daydreams that it was surreal.

"This is too weird, Thompson. Just find the cat and turn the light off, quick." Gina shook her head to clear it and then knelt down to stick her head under the bed. There was Butch showing his back to her. She reached in and let the cat get accustomed to her and then gently picked him up. He seemed very amiable to a female stranger. Gina was glad he hadn't decided to take her hand off. "Are you talking to yourself?" asked Ken. He'd come quietly, too quietly for her to hear, into the room and was practically standing at her elbow. Gina jumped and Butch growled

in protest, jumping from her arms.

"Yes," Gina sighed. "I talk to myself. I grew up with a brother there with me since the first nano---second. So it's weird, totally weird, to be alone sometimes. Besides," said Gina, quirking a smile, "I think I'm interesting enough to carry on a decent conversation with myself."

Ken laughed. "Yeah, believe it or not, I talk to myself too. I guess a lot of people who live alone do that."

Gina smiled and walked past Ken to the bedroom. She was going to try very hard not to remember the painting on Ken's bedroom wall. If she ever found herself in Ken's bedroom, well, then, she'd just make sure the lights were out. That thought was a bit too much, and Gina swallowed a giggle as she sat on the couch.

The coffee table was set with napkins, cloth no less, frosty beer mugs, a huge platter of nachos dripping with cheese, and picante sauce. Ken put on a CD of some soft jazz, by one of her favorite jazz artists (how did he know?), and folded his big body on the floor. Gina made all the right noises of thanks and unceremoniously dug in.

"I didn't know I was this hungry," she said after a

114

swig of her beer. "And I like your cat." Gina braced her elbow on her knee, mug in hand. "Even if he has been eyeing me suspiciously all evening. You suppose he thinks I'm some sort of interloper?"

"Not with cheese all over your chin."

"Why didn't you tell me?" Gina said, wiping furiously at her

chin.

"I don't mind." Ken reached over and squeezed Gina's hand.

He stopped eating; he stopped doing everything but looking into Gina's eyes. "Have I told you how neat I think your eyes are?" Ken scooted over until his thigh was pressing against Gina's. He put his arm around her shoulders, and looked deeply into her eyes. "But you missed a spot." Gina dissolved into giggles as Ken very studiously wiped her chin with his napkin.

"You are funny, Ken," said Gina.

"No one, I mean no one, has ever said I was funny. I've always been too studious for everyone."

"They just don't appreciate that dry wit. You make me

laugh."

"You make me laugh, too. I haven't done that in a long time.

I appreciate it."

Ken reached down and lightly kissed Gina. He pulled his head back and looked at her, then stroked his finger down the side of Gina's cheek, and leaned forward to kiss her again. Gina felt little tingles course down her spine like static electricity and lodge somewhere in her middle. She moved her body closer and Ken pulled her onto his lap. She wrapped her arms around his neck before she could stop herself and moved closer. Ken's fingers lightly moved up and down her spine, wrapping around her upper arm, squeezing and pulling her closer. Gina's head spun with all the sensations that slammed into her, one after the other. She ignored the voice in the back of her mind that told her to pull back.

The static electricity turned into tension that built a fire that might soon became unbearable. Gina pushed herself into Ken in an attempt to get closer to him. Her self----control began to crumple and evaporate like mist on a sunny morning. Ken's scent and the taste of his mouth and tongue assailed her. Reason and caution were firmly put away. Gina slipped her hand under Ken's sweatshirt, feeling the warmth and smooth texture of his back. She wanted to get closer, to melt into him and become part of him. She felt his want as he pressed against her, running his hand up her arm and kneading at the back of her neck, pushing his hands through her hair. The heat radiating from Ken went straight through Gina's trembling hands and straight to her heart.

Too soon, Ken pulled his head away and stared at her with eyes grown dark and smoky. The corner of his mouth edged up into a lopsided grin.

"Do you want to watch a movie? I've got a copy of Tora, Tora, Tora. I just love seeing those planes go down in flames."

Gina burst out laughing. She leaned forward a bit, bracing her hand against the coffee table, and struggled to stand as gracefully as a woman could, climbing up off the floor.

The Tora, Tora, Tora bit was almost as good as a cold shower. Ken was obviously a champion at knowing how to cool down the situation gracefully.

"No, I think I'll go on home and feed the poor pooch. She's probably wondering where I am. I really enjoyed myself." Gina looked up at him under her lashes, feeling, at that moment, terribly shy and awkward. She'd practically shoved her tongue down the poor guy's throat. She wondered what he thought of her and hoped he didn't decide to put her on the top of his pile of discarded women. Wow, what a visual.

Ken got up from the floor and helped Gina with her coat and walked her to her car. He was such a gentleman. Quickly, he reached over and pecked her on the cheek

"I'll call you soon, okay?"

"Okay. See you soon. I'll give Colleen a big kiss for you."

Gina made her way up the mountain, her mind still reeling from that kiss. Her brain was fuzzy and she floated somewhere outside herself. Why had he called a halt to that kiss? Wasn't she glad that he'd stopped and had left it up to her? Well, maybe.

Ken stood outside in the freezing night, watching Gina's taillights disappear down Executive Drive. He was glad that he'd stopped that incredible kiss. At least he thought he was. Standing out in the cold was almost as good as a cold shower...and did he need one. When she touched his bare skin, he thought he just might go into orbit. He was glad he'd stopped it, no use rushing things. Look what happened last time he'd let himself get carried away. Ken decided he'd just cool his heels for a while. Maybe a long while.

"Ouch!" Gina said furiously after she'd whacked her thumb with a hammer for the third time. She carefully examined her thumbnail. It really looked bad; she probably was going to lose it. What else could happen? She sighed and stepped off the stool, staring glumly at the shower rod she'd completely failed to hang properly. She grumbled all the way to the kitchen as she put her tools away and she continued to grumble as she threw herself onto the couch. She just didn't need to put up that extra shower rod right then and there. She'd been trying to put up a balloon valance over the tub the whole weekend. The added cover on the top of the tub, she hoped, would keep out any drafts that puffed into the tub at the oddest times and kept her shivering during her showers. She looked again at her throbbing, reddened thumb, and wondered if she could get blood poisoning from getting it whacked so much. She shivered.

This just in...Teacher found dead in home from whacking thumb with hammer. Details to come, the TV announcer chortled inside her head.

"Oh, Gina, cut it out! You are a scientist, aren't you? So why the constant daydreaming? Well, you know why. Meeting Ken Armstrong made you let your guard down. It's pretty creepy how passion and emotion can take over the head of a completely rational scientist and send her into a tailspin wrapped in cotton candy. Good grief, now not only am I talking to myself but answering myself. What's next? Tarot cards?

"Hey, that's not a bad idea. I'll just call one of those online psychics and see if it's safe to get involved."

Gina plopped into a new position on the couch, still sucking her thumb, and turned on the TV. It was Sunday, 3:30 p.m., and she knew there'd be plenty of infomercials and old movies on all channels. She flipped through channels until she came to a scene with several women speaking about how great it was to find out about their future through a psychic. Gina picked up the phone and started to dial, but then she slammed the receiver down on the cradle.

"This is ridiculous! What am I doing? If it's going to happen, it's going to happen, and I will not pay bucks out the wazoo for information about it. Now Gina, order yourself a pizza, call your mother, and ask Andy over here tomorrow to fix the valance over the tub. See," she said as she stared at herself in the little decorative mirror that hung on her living room wall. "You have complete control over your life. Right? Right!"

Gina slumped down on the couch as her thoughts tumbled through her head a million miles an hour.

"You know, Thompson," she said aloud, the words echoing around the living room and bouncing off the walls. "Since this man has come into your life, you have been an absolute bundle of nerves. Have you done any research? No. Have you thought of any creative and wonderful lessons to charm your

121

students with? No. Have you even completed the application for the PhD program at the University of Alabama? No, no, no, no, no! Get a grip."

Putting the incessant commentary behind her, Gina pulled on her ski jacket, loaded Colleen into the car, and made her way down the mountain to Madison.

Maybe listening to her niece wail for the next few hours would straighten her brain out. She was so proud of herself. She'd come to terms with her own insanity and squashed it flat. She sang her praises so loudly that she completely forgot she'd ordered a pizza to be delivered to her home.

Chapter Six

Friday night was already and indeed here, and the whole prospect horrified Ken when he realized it. He had dreaded the evening since he'd talked to Uncle Yo in the middle of the week. But he'd gotten his hair cut again, the second time in a month. That was a new and unusual experience. Now, here he was at Michael's with the chic of the chic of Huntsville. His Uncle Yo had set him up and here he was waiting for… Waiting for Godot.

If he admitted it to himself, he'd really much rather be waiting for Gina. He avoided his e----mail and the phone like the plague over the past few days. He was waiting in his pragmatic sort of way, waiting to see what would happen. Waiting to see if his own stubborn self would admit to how he felt about her. Well, it was just too soon to decide how he felt, and he'd be drawn and quartered if he'd rush into anything.

The door opened and in walked a…a woman. Maybe. She had on a long, slinky, very plain black skirt and long----sleeved midriff blouse that buttoned up the front. Her hair was very straight, with eye---shielding bangs, and black. So black it must've been dyed. Her eyes, what he could see of them, were heavily lined in black and the woman wore black eye shadow. The most chilling thing about her was the burnished silver pentagram that she wore around her neck on a black strip of leather.

Ken looked at her for a second, wondering what coven she hailed from. He shook his head and turned around to look inside the restaurant, but felt a tap on his shoulder.

"Hi," a silky, husky, yet overly sweet voice oozed out of the woman with the bangs. "Are you Ken Armstrong?"

"Y----yes," Ken said as he turned quickly and stared into the heavily lined eyes of the witch---like woman he'd just seen. His insides crumbled.

"Well, I'm Susan. So nice of your uncle to fix us up like this."

"Yes, isn't it, though," said Ken, trying to keep the ice from his voice.

Susan reached up and pulled his head down. She smacked a long wet kiss on his lips shoving her tongue roughly into his mouth. Just as quickly, she released him. He staggered back, feeling nauseated. He plastered a smile on his face, and resisted the urge to wipe his mouth. He hoped she wouldn't turn him into a toad.

"I hate suspense," she said, stroking her hand over his chest with pointed crimson red nails. "Now that we know, let's eat fast." She licked her lips in what she must've thought was a provocative manner, but all it did was make Ken's knees feel weak and his stomach fall with a lurch and end up near his feet. He was really hoping that this woman couldn't put a curse on him or something. She looked like she could do it. And she was a kindergarten teacher?

Ken's head didn't stop spinning until the maître d' had seated them. They were both looking over the menu and as Ken regained his equilibrium, he began to sweat. How was he going to get himself out this?

"Will you excuse me?" he said, making a quick

decision. "Hurry back," she purred as she clutched at his sleeve. Ken saw the long nails sharpened into dagger----like ends on each finger. He looked up quickly and forced the corners of his mouth up in a smile as he hurried to the subtly lighted hallway near the restrooms. He had to make the call far out of earshot of the woman sitting at his table. He grabbed his cell, but his fingers fumbled over the numbers so that he had to click off and start again. The phone on the other end ominously rang once, and then it rang yet again. At last, his uncle answered the phone.

"Uncle Yo?"

"Are you enjoying yourself, my boy?"

"Uncle Yo, call this restaurant and get me on the phone. I need to get out of here and you are the only one that can get me out of this mess, the one you put me in, by the way, without looking completely rude. And besides, I think well, maybe she could…"

"Now, now, what is the matter with you, my boy?"

"Look, Uncle Yo," Ken whispered urgently into the receiver, looking over his shoulder anxiously, kicking himself for acting like a complete wuss. "I think she's a witch or something."

"What? What did you say? A witch? A hexen? Ah, really." "Just call the restaurant and have me paged to the phone. I'lltake it from there." Ken plastered a smile on his face before he hung up the phone to return to his table. "Well, Susan, and what do you do? My uncle tells me you're a school teacher?"

A laugh that so closely resembled the cackle of a wicked witch in a child's worst nightmare disrupted the quiet atmosphere of the restaurant. Ken felt the color drain from his face.

"A schoolteacher?" Huge black smudges were left on the white linen napkin as Susan wiped the tears from her eyes. "My motto," she said as she leaned towards Ken conspiratorially, "is keep the grill hot and have plenty of barbecue sauce, for any little unwanted, unsuspecting kiddies that may cross my path." She wrinkled her nose and again melted into gales of laughter at her own disgusting joke. "No, no. I work in an herb shop on the south side of town," she said as she took a drink of her water. "We sell some very unusual combinations that produce all sorts of interesting effects. I have some in my purse," she whispered across the table. "They have wonderful results. If you take them before... you know..." She wrinkled her nose twice.

Ken glanced around, quickly looking to see if something had popped out onto the table.

"Pardon, Monsieur Armstrong, there is a telephone call for you. You will find the telephone near the restrooms."

The waiter held Ken's chair as he got up from the table. Ken nodded to him and then said, "Oh, thank you. Sorry, I'll be back in a minute." Ken got up hurriedly and forced himself not to run from the table.

"Uncle Yo? Look, you and I are going to have a very long talk about this matchmaking stuff. Wait till you hear about this one."

Ken hung the phone up and took a deep breath, and counted to five before he walked sedately back to the table. He leaned down and looked sadly at Susan, his imagined Wicked Witch. "I'm so sorry," said Ken. "My uncle just called and he's had a fall. Just a slight one, I'm sure, but I'll have to go over there and check it out. Please continue your dinner. The bill has already been paid."

"Oh poo! Well, can't you just come back after you've

checked on him? I know these things happen." "

"No, I don't think so."

"Well, sweetie, you've got my number, call me sometime."

There, she did it again. She wrinkled her nose twice in quick succession and Ken was sure he was about to turn into a wart---- covered toad.

Ken waved as he left, trying desperately not to run. "Yeah," he said under his breath. "I'll call you the very day you start wearing white."

"Really, Gina, the guy's a knockout. You'll have a blast." "Okay, Janice, I'm absolutely worn down. Bring on Apollo."

"Why do you continually reference mythological gods? Are you hoping for one?" Gina was at her parent's home when she'd taken this call about the big fix-up date that supposedly her brother-in-law had set up from Janice. Her mother was standing, expectantly, with her hands clasped together and a little smile across her face. Gina, frowned, not sure what exactly was up with her mother as she stood by and listened to her daughters' conversation.

No, just a knight in shining armor with dark hair and violet----blue eyes, Gina thought. "Gimme a break, Janice. I'm just being persnickety."

"I always said that if you showed everyone how brainy you were that it would get you continually into trouble."

"Were you brought up during the mid ages? You know, the days when women had to hide their intelligence is long past."

Gina looked at her mother; the older woman was still wringing her hands and anxiously looking at Gina. Now, what is going on here?

Janice's voice intruded. Now, his name is Bill, Bill Graves, and he'll meet you at the Steak and Ale at 7:30 p.m."

"Yes. This had better be good. I know where you live, you know. And this is absolutely the last time. I hope you understand that, because the next one you fix me up with will get stood up, by me." Gina hung up amid

Janice's hoots of laughter.

"Mom, what is going on? Why are you wringing your hands and why do you have that worried look on your face?"

"It's nothing, dear. It's just that your dad and I wanted to speak with you before you left this evening."

"Okay."

With feelings bordering on dread, Gina approached her father's study with her mother following close behind.

"Frank," her mother called.

"Hummmm."

Her father did not look up from the complicated weather map from NOAA on his monitor. "Frank," she said, shaking his arm."Frank, we need to talk to Gina, see she's here."

Her father looked up and gave her a smile. "Hi, pumpkin, what's up?"

"I have no idea, Dad. Maybe you can get Mom to tell you. I personally think she and Janice are in cahoots about something."

"Really, Gladys. Can't you just let Gina be? The two of you do not have enough to do, because if you did, you'd stop pestering the poor girl. I heard from Bob, your son-in-law, how messed up that blind date Janice set Gina up with.

Frank stood and hugged his wife, while he mouthed to Gina," don't worry, I got your back."

Gina smiled, but ducked her head to keep her mother, who had turned around now, from seeing her.

"All right, Gladys, spill it."

"Janice and I are concerned that Gina has no personal relationships, except the dog, of course,…"

"And Andy," Gina interjected.

"Yes, of course, but I mean really, your 31 years old and you live alone on top of the mountain, and …"

"Mom, Mom, I live on the mountain because I need to be close to the planetarium for my work. Get it?"

Her mother shrugged and looked down, obviously embarrassed. "But…"

"No buts." Gina felt like waggling her finger in her mother's face. "When I want to have a relationship,

I'll go look for one, okay? I am a busy woman. Along with everything else, I am applying to U.A. for the Ph.D. program. Janice has been the biggest pain, Mom. I do not want the two of you in my personal life now. Not now, not ever." Gina tried, but could not help the aggravation from coming out with each and every word. Her mother looked crestfallen and Gina reached out and gave her a fierce hug. "Mom, I am a busy woman with lots of responsibilities. I think Dad is right, neither of you have enough to do."

"I'm sorry, I promise no more meddling. And I'll call Janice off, too."

Yeah, right, and if I believe that then I'm sure there's a tract of land in Florida with lots of mosquitoes that someone will sell me.

Gina hugged both her parents.

"I have to go." As she pulled on her jacket and clipped on Colleen's lead and then looked up at her mother. "Why don't you go to the hospital and read stories to the pediatric patients or rock the babies in the neonatal ward. You'd be very good at that, you are such a loving Mom. I love you, but I've got to get home. Tus." She said, the parting word in German had now become part of her vocabulary. "Well, uh, bye."

And before long she was making her way up the dark, cold mountain to her home and her wonderful kerosene heater.

Janice dialed the number she had scotch taped to the receiver of her phone. "Hello, it's Janice."

"Oh, hello, my dear. And how is the plan coming along?" "The bigger question is how did it go the other night with

Ken?"

"Oh, my dear, I think I successfully scared the Pissen right

out of him. He was such a funny calling me to rescue him when he was at the restaurant. I think I felt a little sorry for him. But, just a little."

"That's terrific. Plan B is in effect, and I think with a little nudging from the two of us, they will be ready to call shopping around, quits."

Jimmy and Renee stood against the wall in the hallway leading to the teacher's offices in the science wing and giggled like preschoolers.

"Did you see Ms. Thompson at NASA the other day?"
"Uh----huh. What about it?"

"Oh, men! Didn't you see the way Mr. Armstrong was looking at her? "

"No, I guess I didn't."

"Jimmy, you are hopeless. Did you see the way they were looking at one another? They looked all goofy----eyed. The question is, can we do anything, anything at all, to bring the two of them together?"

"Renee, if Ms. Thompson was okay with Mr. Armstrong, I guess she'll do okay without any help from us. I mean, do you really see yourself as a matchmaker?"

"Jimmy, don't you want them to be as happy as we are?" she said. She nudged Jimmy into a stairwell away from prying eyes and kissed him soundly.

"Well, sure, but... what are we supposed to do?" he said, pushing himself away from Renee as he took a deep breath.

"I've got it all figured out —we'll invite him to our class trip to the planetarium. The trip is at night, so when the program ends, he'll be forced to see her alone."

"You really think this will work?" "Sure, it's how I got you, isn't it?"

———————————•••●•••———————————

From: Jimmy Henderson <Hendj@triangle.Lr.net>
To: Ken Armstrong

RE: von Braun planetarium "Dear Mr. Armstrong,

I got your e----mail address from Ms. Thompson. She figured you wouldn't mind if we had some additional questions about the paper.

The class is going to the planetarium this next Monday. Would you like to meet us there? I know the other kids would like to meet you. And if you're up to it, they'll ask you tons of questions. You can e----mail Ms. Thompson about it or you can just meet us at the planetarium at six on Monday.

I sure do appreciate everything you did for Renee and me last week.

Hope to see you Monday. Jimmy Henderson"

"Dear Jimmy,

I will be delighted to see the planetarium show with your class this coming Monday. Don't say anything to your teacher. We'll call it a surprise.

Ken"

"Wow, what a surprise. Looks like we're barking up the right tree," said Renee as she read the computer screen over Jimmy's shoulder.

"Well, how do you know it's the right tree? Maybe she hates him."

"I know how to find out," said Renee as she pulled Jimmy by the hand to their teacher's office where they politely knocked.

"Come in," Gina called. "Oh, Jimmy, Renee, how's the project coming?"

"Fine, Ms. Thompson," said Jimmy, and Gina noticed the furtive glances Jimmy gave to Renee, and she was nudging him with her elbow. "We were wondering…"

"Wondering what?"

"About this guy Ken Armstrong," said Jimmy, the words tumbled out in a rush. "He seems really nice."

Gina heaved a big sigh, and she knew she had a dopey dreamy----eyed look spreading across her face.

"Yes, he does seem nice, and helpful. I never thought in my wildest imaginings that he'd help the two of you so much. I'm so glad."

"Gee, Ms. Thompson, you look all dre—"

Jimmy started to say as Renee nudged him hard in the ribs.

"Yes," said Gina with one raised brow and a no---- nonsense look on her face. "I do really like him. But he is a man, you know... ah," said Gina. "Well, never mind."

"Well, Ms. Thompson, if there's any way I can help— " began Jimmy just before he got another whack in the ribs from his girlfriend's elbow.

"Okay, you two, thanks for the pep talk, now don't you have a class to go to?"

Her two students waved as they hurried from the

office. Gina leaned back in her squeaky chair that listed to one side and slipped deep into her favorite daydream.

A shaggy----haired man with beautiful eyes and a disarming smile stood off in the distance. He wore a suit of armor of dull black, the helm tucked neatly under his arm. The black warhorse he sat upon danced about nervously, but he was in full control of the big, beautiful animal. He bowed slightly and extended his lance, as though he was waiting for her. He asked for a favor that he could take with him into battle. He leaned forward, his eyes hovering mere inches from her face. She could feel the warmth of his breath and —

Bring!

Gina jumped as the bell rang for third period and reverberated through the walls of her little cubicle, signaling that it was time for her physical science class.

"In the name of Copernicus, I've got to cut this out. This simply will not do," Gina chided herself under her breath as she grabbed her book satchel and started the maneuvering process around the influx of students moving the other way. "I am too practical and too smart to sit here and daydream about a man that 'doesn't know me from Adam.' Well, maybe he knows me a little. We have shared some pretty neat times, and other things." Gina felt herself smirk, remembering that incredible kiss they had shared in his apartment.

Gina growled at herself, get a grip! She slammed her books on the top of the black lab sink, she used as a desk during her classes. Things were just getting out of hand, and she must stop it right here and now; she just had to stop the never----ending daydreams.

The students of her ninth grade physical science class filed into her room, chattering loudly as they made themselves comfortable and got their books out. A piece of balled----up paper launched from somewhere in the middle of the room sailing toward the front. Gina caught it easily one----handed and looked unemotionally at her class. Not a sound was heard except the late bell fading into the distance.

"Thanks for the extra paper. I can always use some scrap. Turn to page one hundred seventy----three and we will begin by discussing the questions at the bottom of the page. Robert, read number one."

"'What are the properties of volcanic ash?' Well, I think that, uh…"

Gina drifted into a fog and in her mind the knight leaned down from his saddle, his lips brushing hers, and didn't realize that Robert had finished his answer until he roughly cleared his throat.

She shook her head abruptly, forcing her mind on the here and now.

"Okay everyone, grab your lab partners and start with question 5 on page 157. Fill in the answers in your lab books and turn them in at the end of class."

At first, the students murmured their surprise at the 'by the book' Miss Thompson changing direction in the middle of class. After a moment they got themselves organized and Gina watched as her students milled around the class, but her mind was on only half the class and the other half was on thoughts of Ken. Could she write an equation that would prove that love at first sight was concrete and not just an idea or an emotion? Gina took a pencil and jotted down some numbers, but then her eagle teacher's eye trained onto a gaggle, and that's the only way she could describe them, of girls standing near the fish tanks on the far side of the room. Oh, was she ever that young and foolish? Most probably, but it was difficult to remember specifics, just that now, even the thought of some of her antics made her blush with embarrassment. How the human race developed past the puberty years intact after all these millennia was amazing to her, and she was a scientist.

She nonchalantly wandered closer to the giggling gaggle of girls. Watching the other students as she passed each of their stations while she listened to the chatter.

"And do you know what she said? She told me that Steve was just her 'friend'." One of the girls said using air quotes around the word friend. "Of course, I didn't believe her. She is such a be-ot-ch. I mean..." And before Gina could chastise the student for using that form of the word 'bitch', the girl's elbow caught the end of one of the large fish tank covers and the thin sheet of plastic went hurdling through the air, spraying water over the girls before it landed with a loud plop in the middle of the floor. And right along with the cover a large gray guppy was propelled onto the head of the girl closest to the tank.

Promptly the girls, all of them, screamed. Miss Fish Head screamed louder and longer than anyone else, batting the air around her head. "Get it off, get it off." The fish hit the floor with another resounding splat.

"Pipe down, I'll get the fish, no one move, you might step on it." Gina warned, raising her voice to be heard above the throng.

The entire class, strained to get nearer the poor flopping fish while Gina grabbed the first of the nets near the tanks. The guppy was large, for a guppy, and flopped about violently. Gina went to her knees.

"Oh, crap! Uh, sorry, Robert, quick, grab the other net! The two of them tried several times before she grabbed the fish, which promptly jumped out of the net. She got the fish again. Her shoulder collided with Robert's when she stood, and the fish almost made it onto the floor again, but Robert reached over and clapped his net on the top of Gina's. And this time, they successfully got the guppy into the tank and the cover back on.

"Now, go sit down, and you girls, clean up this mess. You," she said as she pointed to the 'fish head girl'. "Go to the restroom and clean up, you're going to

143

smell like a fish tank."

"Oh, can I go with her," one of the girls asked.

"No, you may not. Now, everybody, SIT DOWN." The students milled about finally getting into their seats. The girls cleaning up the fish tank, weren't so lucky. They had lots of water to mop up and they weren't going anywhere till it was clean. "Everyone," Gina said. She glanced at the clock. Thank God there were only ten more minutes of class. "Just do something constructive and don't say A WORD, and I mean a word."

Books were pulled out and read and notebooks scribbled in, and Gina took a whiff of the sleeve of her sweater. She decidedly smelled like a guppy. Gross. She'd have to leave school as soon as the bell rang to shower and change. Seven more minutes of class. Gina took up the equation she'd started on the proof of love at first sight. She messed around, trying to get the equation to balance not sure if she'd even put remotely in the right parameters. Surely, there was a way to prove it, ah love.

It was 6:45 p.m. Friday night and it was time for her to leave her little house and drive to Huntsville for the infamous date Janice had arranged for her. She'd much rather stay home and watch an old black----and----white movie. Hepburn and Tracy were always her favorites. She could never fathom, though, how Katharine Hepburn always knew that Spencer Tracy was Mr. Right. Maybe things were less complicated back in the non---- computer age, and especially if everything was in black and white.

Gina pointed her little green car down the mountain, muttering furiously at the absurdity of her sister's matchmaking. Janice could be overbearing sometimes, especially when she took this big sister thing a little too far.

Just for a second, Gina. Imagine the headlines:

This just in... Baby sister, teacher, murders older sister because of eternal, infernal matchmaking: Gina Thompson, a teacher at Grissom High School was arrested Saturday for strangling her big sister. "I couldn't help it," Thompson was reported to have said. "I plead temporary insanity."

Well, that was a really satisfying split----second

moment, Gina thought. She forced her mind on the inevitable bad evening to come, and let her favorite daydream take over.

He was big and beautiful in his burnished black suit of armor, his helm a under his arm. The gold Fleur De Lis emblazoned on his shield gleamed brightly in the sunlight. No, no, he was after all half German, so the decoration on the armor was an eagle with outstretched wings. His high----cheek boned face framing those marvelous violet----blue eyes stared at her. There was a twinkle in his eye as he smiled. He leaned down from the back of the huge shining black warhorse and his lips just barely brushed hers. A tingle coursed up her spine, and she sighed deeply, wishing… wishing... He was such a hunk with that wonderful scruffy hair and angled chin and wide chest that looked as though it was just made for her head to snuggle against.

Before she knew it, her daydream ended as she arrived at the restaurant. Her hands trembled slightly as she drove into the packed parking lot. She noted with some satisfaction how many cars were parked in the popular bistro. Typically on Friday and Saturday nights, just about every place downtown was packed with the high tech crowd who toiled in Huntsville's rich engineering and aeronautical industries. At least she'd get a good meal out of this. A good meal with no dirty dishes to wash.

She hurried into the lobby and stood facing the gas log fireplace.

"Gina?"

Gina turned slowly, and her stomach dropped to the bottom of her feet. She had always prided herself on being an open----minded person, not prone to making fast judgments about people's looks, but the man that stood in front of her left her breathless. Maybe a better word would be speechless.

He was no more than three inches taller than she was. This left her with a very strange impression of staring him in the eyebrows. There was only one, eyebrow that is, and it was thick, brown, and made of wiry hair. The wiry hairs across the bridge of his nose stood out a few inches from his head, as though he were a porcupine about to let loose a few quills. The man had light blue eyes that were slightly slanted in, and ears that pointed just enough at the top so that he looked like a gnome. Or maybe a troll that made his home in a snarl of weeds under a bridge somewhere.

Oh, Ken Armstrong, where are you when I need you?

"Ah, are you Gina?" the man asked. He rocked back and forth on his heels with his hands crammed into his pockets. He leered at her, stared pointedly at her breasts, and practically drooled. Mr. Bill obviously didn't get out into polite society enough.

"Yes, are you Bill?"

"Janice told me all about you. Well, well, you are quite a looker, sure glad she got me fixed up and all."

The man's accent reminded Gina of the last cotton farmer father, she'd had a teacher's conference with. Not maligning cotton farmers, but wasn't this man some kind of professional math something or other?

"Well, thank you." Gina pushed aside the edge that was about to form on her attitude. What would happen if her brother---- in----law found out that she was nasty to this man that worked in his office? She'd have to explain herself and watch her wonderful brother----in----law get his feelings hurt.

"We should go to our table...now," Gina said as she tried to move the leering man into the dining room.

148

Perhaps there, she hoped, his attention would be diverted to other things besides this overt concentration of her.

As they were escorted to their seats, Bill put his hand on Gina's waist, and let it drift a little too low. Gina walked quickly ahead, removing her hip from the offensive hand. When they were seated at the table and Gina scooted into the booth, but the man had the audacity to reach under the table and tweak her knee.

Gina narrowed her eyes at Bill and then, very deliberately, got up and moved to the seat as far away from him as she could. Feeling completely bereft of any good feeling for her dinner partner, Gina chided herself: Come on, Gina, the guy is probably really sweet. Just give him a chance.

"Well, Gina, tell me all about yourself."

"I teach at Grissom High School. I teach science, Earth and Physical, and —"

"Well, that's too bad. All the sex and violence in school these days." Bill's eyes began to shine, and not in a good way. Gina sat back in her seat and stared at the man. What was he driving at?

"It's outrageous," he continued.

The man really leered now, to some scene he saw in his own head. His gold eyetooth winked in the candlelight and his mono eyebrow twitched in and out. The wiry hairs in the center, especially the longest one that was dead center, moved up and down, up and down, until it looked like it was doing a little dance. Gina shook her head and looked away; the man's dancing eyebrow, shouldn't there be two, seemed to do its best to hypnotize her.

"And may I ask, have you caught any of your students… um, you know?"

Gina felt the color drain from her face. Was the man asking about the sex lives of her students? She didn't know anything about their sex lives. She routinely prayed that they had none at all.

"Bill, I hardly think—"

"Yes, yes, that's all right. Now, let me tell you all about me."

The man sat back, his eyes closed, a look of rapture on his face. Apparently, he thought he was really something.

"I'm a CPA and head of the…"

Gina's mind switched off. She prided herself on the ability to tune out loud, obnoxious noises, a necessary survival tactic for anyone teaching public school. This man really got to her. She began to successfully space out until she felt a clammy hand reach for her knee. She stood so fast that her chair nearly turned over. "Will you excuse me a minute?" she said and left the table without looking back. She walked to a short corridor with water fountains, a couch, a table arranged artfully with silk flowers, and the restrooms. She reached into her purse, grabbed her cell, and punched in the speed dial for her sister Janice.

"Janice, you call me at this restaurant right this minute. And if you ever have the audacity to fix me up again, I will disown you. Do you understand me?"

"Isn't your date with Bill working out?" came a too, too innocent sing songy voice. "The guy is an unbelievable lecher. How could you? I will never speak to you again. Do you understand?" Gina felt her face grow hot and she was relatively sure that she might have a stroke on the spot. "Except when you call this restaurant in the next three minutes to tell me that there is an emergency and that I must go home. Is that understood?"

"Now, Gina, don't take that schoolteacher tone with me." There was an audible sigh from the other end of the phone.

"Yes, I'll call. And I'll never get you fixed up again."

"Well, thank the heavens for small favors. I mean it, Janice. As soon as I hang up, your call had better be under three minutes."

"Okay, under three minutes."

Gina took a huge breath, and rested her for head against the wall. How did she get herself into these things? No more. No more, exclamation point, from now on. If she wanted anyone, she would find him herself. As she turned to leave, the daydream that had taken up residence inside her head played yet again, like an old---- fashioned vinyl record stuck in the same groove.

"Oh, Gina, give it up," she said aloud. She made her way back to the table, the clammy hands, and the leering gold eyetooth of her date.

"Sorry. Have you ordered?"

"I took the chance and ordered you a tea, sweet, of course."

"Yes, of course," mumbled Gina into her menu. She hated sweet tea, even if everyone else in the South loved it.

A waiter came to the table, looking anxiously at Gina. "Miss Thompson?"

"Yes?"

"There's a phone call for you. Will you follow me, please?"

Gina got up hurriedly and followed the man to the telephone at the hostess station.

"Janice?"

"Yes, it's me," said a tried and tired voice on the other end of the receiver. "There's an emergency," continued the mono----toned voice. "Come home at once." Click. Could Janice have spoken any slower or sounded any duller? It was almost funny. Almost. Gina promised herself she would laugh as soon as she pulled into her garage.

"Oh, Bill, I'm so sorry. It seems there is a family

emergency and I must dash off."

"Would you like me to come wait with you?"

"Oh, no, no. Please finish your dinner. Thank you so much for the iced tea." It was all Gina could do to keep from running to the exit. She reached the door before Bill could get up from his seat and say anything. Her hand shook, but still she managed to insert the key into the door of her car. She was decidedly going to kill Janice for this.

Later, after Gina had changed into her sweats, made herself a cup of tea, no sugar, and eaten a hot dog, she logged on to her e---- mail. Before she could think about what she was doing, she had typed in Ken's e----mail address and written:

"Dear Ken,

Had the worst, strangest, enter----appropriate----adjective night of my life tonight.

So, how are you?"

Gina pushed send before she could change her mind and then settled down on the couch. She picked up a great romantic suspense that she'd started that week. She kept wishing it were a medieval romance. It was so easy to imagine Ken as the hero.

Chapter Seven

"But I just don't know what that has to do with anything.

Maybe he just wants to see the planetarium show."

"Oh, Jimmy, how can you be so immature? The reason he's coming is so he can see Ms. Thompson. Don't you get it?"

"Well," said Jimmy as he sat at his computer terminal, scratching his head and wondering, "If he wants to come see Ms. Thompson, then how come we're supposed to keep it a secret?"

"Oh, men. How do you guys make it without us women helping you out?" teased Renee. She reached up to ruffle Jimmy's big shock of brown hair. "Now, what we'll have to do is to be real nonchalant and kind of make sure we're near the door when he comes in so we can get them to sit together. Just leave it to me, okay? I'll take care of everything."

———•••●●••———

Later that evening, twenty students and Gina made their way in the dark on the rocky path from the parking lot to the planetarium. There were no outside lights and several of the students, including Gina, had brought flashlights to keep from tripping in the dark.

"Everyone all right?"

"Sure, Ms. Thompson," her favorite student, John, joked. "We will delightedly fall on our backsides to get up this silly hill to see the planetarium show."

"Hey," postured someone else amid puffing students and the sound of crunching gravel. "You stepped on me."

"Oops, sorry."

Gina smiled to herself, enjoying the camaraderie of all these intelligent youngsters still being teenagers. The heavy wooden double doors screeched open as the kids filed in.

"Well, I see you all are here," said the very

knowledgeable gray----haired lady curator. "How have y'all been since your last visit? I think we have some real surprises for you. Our astronomer is going to show you some pictures taken recently by the Mars Probe and then we will have a question----and---
-answer period."

Amid oohs and ahs, the class shuffled about and found their seats. Gina stood near the back of the circular amphitheater making sure all the students were seated and enough flashlights were handed out so that they could take the notes she required as part of a class project. She was surprised to see that Jimmy and Renee, usually the first ones seated and ready to listen, were loitering around the doors. She frowned, wondering what they were about when the outer door opened and in stepped Ken Armstrong.

Gina's quick intake of breath caused her to cough and sputter and keep her hand over her mouth as she quickly assessed what she was wearing. Had she bothered to comb her hair or put on lipstick and mascara? Rats! She wasn't expecting Mr. Right to come ambling through the door. He looked like a glossy color advertisement for elegant men's clothing, and here she was in a light blue (not her color) baggy sweater, blue jeans that had seen better days, and sneakers. At least the planetarium was always dark. The last two times that she'd been there, she'd tripped on the way from the parking lot and snagged her stocking and slacks. This time she thought she'd be sensible and go for comfort. And now Ken showed up in a turtleneck sweater and a tweed sport coat, looking like the dashing English Lord or something. Well, she just could not win.

Ken strode purposefully up the aisle, never taking his eyes from her, a slight smile at the corners of his mouth. Gina's heart beat entirely too fast.

The blood surged through Ken's veins when he saw her, and did a little tattoo thrumming against his temples. Ken had come to see Gina, be with her, and told Jimmy and Renee to keep the fact of his coming a secret. "Damn the torpedoes, full speed ahead." Gina wasn't expecting him and maybe he felt he still had to check her out, make sure she was who he thought she was. Gorgeous, stunning, she took his breath away. Even in that awful light blue sweater. Ken took her hand and inhaled deeply of Gina, his head whirling with the steady bump, bump, bump of his heart. He gazed into those beautiful, dark brown eyes and it almost undid him. He remembered where they were. They were surrounded by high school students and planetarium staff. But he grappled with the desire to throw her over his shoulder and carry her off like a caveman. He was much too pragmatic for such base feelings—he thought, maybe.

"Had a lousy blind date, huh?" Ken quipped. "I'll tell you about mine with the Wicked Witch after the lecture." Gina raised her eyebrows. "I'm not kidding. I mean, she was literally a witch." Gina giggled helplessly, and most uncharacteristically, as they made their way to the seats that Renee had saved for them.

As the planetarium show unfolded, followed by a lecture and question----and----answer period, the amount of detail Gina revealed of her knowledge of cosmology made Ken uncharacteristically proud. As Gina asked the lecturer about the alignment of lenses in the Hubble Telescope and its ultimate angle to pick up the Mars Probe, Ken felt slightly dimwitted.

Well, Ken, ponder this: if we do get together, there will never be a lack of anything for us to talk about. Gina couldn't believe it. Ken had come to see her and she felt a little quiver of excitement. Perhaps he'd made his mind up about getting involved with her. Perhaps, he decided to go with it. Her dreams had decidedly become filled with knights. Knights that looked just like Ken. Maybe she could go with it, too. The knight with those violet----blue eyes, so vivid in her constant daydreams, had to be some sort of omen, didn't he? It was getting harder and harder to concentrate on what she needed to do without the daydreams intruding.

Was that a chemical reaction that had knocked her flat the first moment she laid eyes on him? She'd look it up on her favorite search engine — love at first sight — surely, there was a scientific answer. Gina had looked at him out of the corner of her eye, just a quick peek. His eyes were so luminous, dark and smoky. She could feel the palpable tension that surrounded them. And how could she break this tension? Maybe she'd look up that as well. As the lecture continued, Gina got so lost in the stars that she almost forgot he was there. Almost.

Ken held Gina's hand as the class filed and, in some cases, stumbled up the path to the parking lot. It wasn't as cold as it had been, so she had no excuse to walk as close to Ken as she could. She said very few words to the class as they started their engines and slowly drove out of the parking lot. When the class was gone, Gina and Ken made their way to his Jeep. Gina started to walk to her car, but he turned to her and lightly brushed his fingers across her cheek. The touch sent cold shivers up her spine and at the same time caused the blood to rush to the parts she wouldn't think about right now.

"Want to go get a cup of coffee?" he asked. "Sure. Where are we going?"

"I don't know, you pick."

Gina thought for a second. Where would you like to be alone with Ken? Well, don't let your mind go too far afield.

"I know a place in town that makes a really good cappuccino and we can sit at the bar."

"Sounds good to me. Leave your car here and I'll drive you back up to get it."

"Are you sure? Isn't that out of your way?"

"Nah, I don't have to be at work until nine. I'll bet your day starts a lot earlier than that."

"Yeah. I have to be there at 7:15."

"God, that's uncivilized."

Gina climbed into the cab of the Jeep and Ken pulled the seat belt securely around her and then he stopped and looked up at her, his gaze unreadable. He stretched his upper body over quickly and pecked her on the cheek before he shut the door and walked around the car to his side. Gina took a shaky breath, willing her mind to stop racing as fast as her heart. They drove in silence down the mountain to the city.

The Italian restaurant was crowded, even for a Monday night, but the bar was almost deserted. They sat under a big green umbrella festooned with silk flowers, as though the tables were outside at a café, and ordered their drinks from the bartender.

"What did you order?"

"Fra Angelica. I think it's French, or maybe Italian. My mother always had a bottle of this and a bottle of schnapps in the house. Sometimes, when I felt depressed or missed my dad or something, she'd give me a little glass of it. It's so smooth and sweet and has hazelnuts and. It almost reminds me of her, it's, you know, comforting."

"I'm sorry she passed away. I would've liked to have known

her."

"Oh, she was funny, and very wise, a lot like Uncle Yo without the gruffness. I have this drink sometimes when I want to feel close to her. Now," he said after he had a sip. He turned his sharp gaze and his complete attention on Gina. "Tell me about your parents."

"My mother is a housewife, basically from the old school, can't understand why I'm not married with a bunch of kids by now. I do have two sisters that are married. Actually, one is divorced and she and her daughter live with my parents. And you've met Andy. My dad teaches at the University of Alabama at Huntsville. He's due to retire soon and then he'll probably go fishing every day."

"What does he teach?"

"Meteorology, and he heads the research department that they have at the University."

"That's too cool," said Ken as he put down his glass and looked intently at his shoes for a moment. He looked up at Gina and smiled. "Did I tell you that Andy came to see me a couple of weeks ago?"

"Andy did?"

"Yeah, he ordered a pizza and brought a twelve---pack and he sat me down and we watched the Auburn----Tennessee game."

"What?"

"Yeah, if you want to know the truth, I think he was checking me out."

"Checking you out?"

"You know, the 'worthy of my twin sister' routine."

Gina felt the blood rush to her face. That little weasel, she'd get him.

"Hey," grinned Ken. "Don't worry about it. I enjoyed myself, and he brought the pizza and beer, so what more could I ask for?"

"I'll bet Janice put him up to it. She's been trying to marry me off for years. And you should see the absolute creeps she fixes me up with." Gina shuddered and felt heat rush to her face and all the way down to her toes; it was anger mixed with embarrassment, and she knew she was glowing by now. The lighting was subtle in the bar and she was glad of it.

"Please, Gina, don't worry about it. I think it is really nice that you have brothers and sisters that want you to be happy. I don't have any brothers, sisters, aunts, or grandparents, so I can't begin to imagine someone interfering in my life like that. Wait, wait, Uncle Johann does the same thing. I just don't have a busy body under the age of eighty messing with my love life.

"Now, tell me where you went to school, what your degree is in, and all that vital stuff, okay?" Ken reached across the bar and squeezed Gina's hand.

Slowly, Gina felt the flush from her face recede. She took a deep breath before she started to speak again. Her family! What she wouldn't give to have one relative like Ken. Things would be so quiet and calm, no more ratty nephews loading toys with firecrackers, putting them inside your hats, or little toys sabotaging your feet as you walked across the floor. No more nieces wailing in your ear, or big sisters fixing you up with Jack the Ripper. If she had to give up some of the members of her noisy, obnoxious family, whom would she give up? Hmm… that's something to think about. It took only a fraction of a second to decide she wouldn't be able to give up any of them. Rats. She was just stuck with them.

Gina began to tell Ken an abbreviated version of her adult life. He listened intently, and inside his mind a tiny thought niggled at him and wouldn't be silenced. It would be terrific to have brothers, sisters, nieces, and nephews. Gina had all the luck. She had a family. No matter how he loved him, things could get lonely sometimes for a guy with only a grouchy old uncle for his entire family.

"Ken, are you going to work at NASA until you retire?" "Who knows? If the government budget keeps shrinking the way it is now, maybe we'll close up shop someday. Maybe I'llbe able to work for one of the private contractors, like SpaceX. Well, probably not. The guys over there talk about it sometimes. I don't know, maybe I'd like to get my PhD and teach in college."

"Huh, really? That's how I envisioned my life's plan."

Ken laughed with Gina. He thought he'd like to hear her laugh a whole lot more. He reached over and held her hand. The warmth of his fingers in her hand made her tingle all over.

"Look at the time, it's almost midnight, no wonder the bartender keeps giving us dirty looks."

They settled into their coats and walked to the counter where Ken paid the bartender. Gina smiled when she saw him give the patiently waiting bartender a large tip before they made their way out the door.

"Oh, I'll never make it tomorrow." "You could call in sick."

"Ken, you do not understand the workings of the teenage mind, no matter how intelligent they are. They knew I had a date with you after the lecture and if I don't show up tomorrow, they will assume the worst."

168

"Or the best."

Gina laughed out loud "Yes, or the best."

Ken pulled into the parking lot at the planetarium next to Gina's car and got to the passenger side before Gina could unfasten her seat belt. He held her hand as she stepped out of the Jeep and walked her to her car.

"Thanks for tonight. It was wonderful finding out all aboutyou. wonderful It was finding out all about you too."

Ken pulled Gina close as his mouth descended to meet hers.

Her hands reached for him inside his jacket and pulled him close. The cold wind whipped around the couple locked in their passionate embrace. For the first time in months, Gina wasn't cold. His kiss was heady and her head reeled with his touch and taste. His mouth on hers drove every thought from her head as his hands on her body moved with excruciating deliberation, touching, but not touching. Wanting him to touch, but still not touching. She felt a sigh escape his mouth and reverberate into hers. Her mouth opened seemingly of its own accord and she felt him shudder as her tongue touched his and for just a moment, he seemed to melt into her.

And then he pulled away. He still held her very close, his head cocked to one side looking at her with that crooked little smile. Gina felt herself smile, but she ducked her head. She wanted to grin from ear to ear and crow like a rooster, but she knew she had to keep her demeanor. She cleared her throat and then looked up.

"Well, Ken, thanks for the, how many cappuccinos did I have? Three? And thanks for coming tonight."

"You're welcome. Now, you better get to bed, you old schoolmarm."

She saw a smile and then he pecked her cheek before he made his way back to the Jeep. He waved as he waited for her to get into her car and start the engine. He climbed into the Jeep and started it after she'd reached the exit to the parking lot. All the way down the mountain to Gina's house, he followed. She kept looking in her rearview mirror wondering that she dreamed the whole wonderful evening, but after she climbed out of her car in the garage, she turned and saw that he was still there, watching over her. She waved brightly, but he didn't leave until she'd opened the door that led into the house and closed the garage with the automatic door opener. Gina leaned against the door, breathing, just breathing. Wow, what a gentleman. Could she ever get used to him treating her with such deference? Yes, she decided, she could.

Gina spent the next day, yawning hugely behind her hand and drinking as much coffee as her stomach could take. Her astronomy students seemed to be grown----up enough not to spread her liaison with Ken around school. She was happy for that. People, in general, and teenagers in particular, could really be a pain sometime.

The worst thing about the last few weeks of the Ken invasion was that she could feel herself slipping into that dreamy----eyed, goofy state called love. It was too soon, too soon, and she couldn't let herself drool over Ken when she had so much to do for herself.

Gina had bimonthly hair appointments on Tuesday. She'd speak to Tammy, her wonderful hairdresser, about the whole matter. Hairdressers and bartenders, they sure knew how to listen.

Tammy was only five or six years older than Gina, but she seemed to have the knowledge of the sages about life.

Finally, agonizingly, the day drew to a close, and Gina made her way to the little beauty shop in the mall near her house.

"Hey, girl. You look tired. Have you been burning the candle at both ends again?"

"Well, not exactly. There is something that I'd like to talk you about, though."

"Fire away. I've caught a bunch of stories from all kinds of clients today. I had a new client in here the other day and he absolutely spilled his guts about his failed marriage. I never saw anything like it before, so tell your old aunt Tammy all about it."

Gina took a deep breath and stared pointedly at Tammy in the mirror. Tammy quirked her eyebrow in question and waited patiently for Gina to continue.

"Well, I've met a man."

"You, girlfriend? You've met a man? Well, that's terrific.

And about time, too."

"But Tammy, what if he treats me like all the rest of them? How can I keep going? I mean, who's got the energy for all of this drama?"

Tammy swung the chair around and pointed a comb under Gina's nose.

"First of all, you can't dig a hole and crawl into it and stay there. Life is out there and you have to live it. Second, you'll never ever find anyone unless you take a chance on love and life. You have to take a leap of faith and unwrap the asbestos you've put around your heart. It's a leap. That's why it's called falling in love. Now," she said as she swung the chair back around with a lurch. "Tell me about this guy."

"He's an engineer and works at NASA." "That's a ten."

"He's awfully good looking, but doesn't seem to know it or care much about it."

"On a scale of one to ten, that's about a fifteen."

"He really acts like he cares about me and he thinks I'm smart and he listens to me when I talk."

"And tell me why you're running away from this guy again?

You're not, are you?"

"And can he kiss!"

"What are you waiting for? Go for it! No, no, maybe I'll divorce Johnny and I'll go after him."

Gina laughed, and the weight she'd been carrying around with her for weeks dissipated like vapor.

Gina walked around the mall lost in thought about Ken, and her inability to decide what she really wanted out of life.

She managed to get herself some dinner at the food court and then wandered through one of the department stores. She bought herself a much----needed pair of shoes, and decided it was time for a new book. Her favorite book store had a terrific romance section and it was time to take some time and peruse.

Gina looked through the books by one of her favorite authors. She had a new book out and it was a medieval. The back cover reads: "Gregory, a knight of King John, knows the new alewife of the castle is not what she seems. She casts a mysterious allure that he needs to investigate. Lady Katherine De'Venchie, a Norman noble woman, has run from her husband and hidden herself in the Castle disguised as a Saxon serf... but why?"

Oh, cool. Looks like good reading. Gina bought the book and drove home, anxious to read and lose herself in the plot.

Maybe, she could see Ken as the knight, Sir Gregory. She really liked those daydreams she kept having, even if she couldn't admit it to herself. Yes, she probably liked them too well, but she knew how important it was to make sure that the daydreams didn't replace reality.

She hadn't heard from Ken all day, but that was okay.

Things moved a little too fast last night.

Please, Gina's prayer went up, no more lousy relationships.

What had Tammy said? "You can't dig a hole and stay in it, you have to live life. It's a leap of faith, that's why they call it falling in love."

Huh, leap of faith my Aunt Fanny. She'd been doing just fine for the past few months with no involvements at all. Now Gina had lots of time to be by herself and work in the house, pay attention to her beloved Colleen, keep up with her students, and study.

The little niggling voice said, "Gina that is a pretty awful life if all you do is work and study and brush your dog." Tough! For the time being, that would be the way it stayed.

By the time Gina had walked Colleen, given her a good brushing, and done her chores, it was almost nine o'clock. She settled down with her book, turned off the heater in case she fell asleep reading, and began.

The book was outstanding and the plot got thicker and thicker, while the beautiful Lady Katherine tried not to fall in love with the handsome, virile Sir Gregory.

"I know just how you feel, kiddo," said Gina as she splashed cold water on her face to keep from falling asleep. The book was just too good to put down. Gina snuggled back down inside her quilt, moved Colleen so the dog lay right on her cold feet, and continued the story.

****

Ken had spent the better part of the day pacing the floor in his cubicle at work, and then the rug in the living room of his apartment. It was past time to decide if he was serious or not about Gina.

He'd gotten a royal razing from his buddy at work. Jeff stood at the entrance to his cubicle, watching him for a few minutes, before starting in on the questions about Gina. The guy just would not lay off. When he told him that he, Jeff, would be delighted to take her out if Ken wasn't interested, Ken showed Jeff the door, or the break in the partition, if you wanted to get technical, about his office, without comment.

Well, for Pete's sake, he knew he was serious. But how serious? Were those wedding bells ringing in his head or was the buzzing in his ears from too much of Uncle Yo's ever----present droning voice?

What if she turned out to be like all of the others? How could he stand it? He would probably go live in a cave if that happened. But how would he ever know unless he tried to make an effort and get to know Gina really well? Life did go on, but that didn't mean he had to open himself up for every infatuation that came along.

Was Gina just another infatuation? No, not really. She was…What was it exactly that she was to him anyway? Ken sat for a few minutes, running his hands through his hair and pulling it until it stood up away from his scalp all the way around like a mohawk. He stifled a groan and looked down at his coffee table, mentally putting away the junk that littered the top but not moving from the couch.

Yeah, so what if he was thirty----two? Hadn't he done all right so far with just Uncle Yo and no one else?

Uncle Yo thought it was time for him to marry. If his mother were alive, she'd wonder what was stopping him.

Ken could imagine her cajoling. She and Uncle Yo would sit him on the couch and their two faces, laced with concern like pictures from someone's old scrapbook, would stare at him. They would reason and badger until they got their way. They were good at that, reasoning and badgering, that is. What if he turned out that way? What if he turned out to be a nag? What if he turned out to be a lousy father, like some Prussian overbearing but well----meaning papa? He planned not to be. Nope, he was going to be a laid----back dad, no stress, no drama. Ken stopped pulling his hair out and sat back on the couch and put his hands over his eyes. Where in the wide world of sports had that come from? Kids? Who said anything about kids?

Ken sat on his couch with a sigh. He could just imagine three or four little redheads running around a spacious home with a nice little garden in back. A scene of perfect domestic tranquility.

What was he doing? Any domestic tranquility daydreams might get completely out of hand.

Better decide, boy----o, exactly what this Gina Thompson means to you. Face it, Ken, you could talk to her for hours, and she isn't always fiddling with her hair or her face and wondering if her lipstick is on straight. All the important things like family seem to be in line with her. So what are you waiting for? Call her, you idiot, and see if she wants to go to dinner or something. No sense in making a commitment now. Especially when you're so chicken.

Ken groaned as he plopped his head back against the wall. Butch jumped onto his lap and began purring, setting his whole lower body in sympathetic vibration. Ken raised his head a mere inch, and cracked one eye open.

"I love you, Butch, but maybe it's time we have somebody else in our lives. What do you think about Gina?" Ken opened both eyes and reached down, pulling Butch up into a semi----hug. "Maybe it's time, you old man, for the two of us to shed our bachelor ways."

Sir Gregory, disguised as Ken, made his way up to the turrets in the moonlight. In the narrow, winding stair, the heavy hilt of his sword scraped against the stairwell. Lady Katherine, disguised as Gina Thompson, dressed only in her shift and lightweight shawl turned and gasped at the sound of the scraping sword. Oh, goodness, it was the Lord of the keep, Sir Gregory… Ken.

"My Lord, I came to catch a breath of fresh air." Lady Katherine pulled the shawl about her, trying to make herself melt into the darkness. Sir Gregory…Ken, strutted up to Lady Katherine, grabbed her, and looked deeply into her eyes. His face loomed larger than life. She knew he was going to kiss her. She could feel the heat of his hands imprint themselves on her arms. He leaned closer and closer, sniffed indignantly, scowled, turned, and left. Lady Katherine's eyes filled with tears and…

Gina awoke with a start, gasping for air. Her heart thumped almost painfully against her chest. She looked about, not sure where she was until she realized she was in her own living room. She had fallen asleep on the couch with the book lying open across her chest and the light from the end table glaring in her eyes. She reached up and touched her face, not surprised that her cheeks were wet with tears.

Gina staggered up into a sitting position, glared at the book, and unceremoniously threw it across the kitchen. In a perfect arc that Michael Jordan would have been proud of, it landed in the kitchen trash. Nothing but net.

"Holy Moly, it's 3:30 a.m. I will never make it tomorrow. I'm calling in sick." Without thinking overly much about her decision, Gina called the voicemail that took messages from teachers who thought they were sick or needed a mental health day.

"That's what I need," said Gina to the bathroom wall. "A mental health day. Good thing I left detailed lesson plans. Those kids will be easier on a sub… or I'll kill 'em, metaphorically speaking." Gina took two nighttime pain relievers, turned off her alarm, and crawled under the covers. Colleen snuggled onto her feet, and Gina drifted off into a dream----filled, restless sleep.

A sharp, painful noise reached down into the fog of Gina's mind. She sat up, with a gasp, only realizing after banging her head on the headboard that the phone was ringing.

"Hello?" "Gina?

"Janice? What's going on?"

"Gina, it's 9:30 in the morning. Why aren't you in school?" "If you thought I was in school, why are you calling me at home?"

Gina heard the exasperation all the way from Athens. "Well, the old lady secretary, you know, Mom's friend, called Mom and said you called in sick."

"Yes, and?"

"Well, we're just all worried about you and we thought..." "Look, Janice," Gina rubbed her eyes with the heels of her hands, feeling the old familiar irritation from her family's overbearing attitude engulf her good sensibilities as her teeth begin to clench together. Briefly, she thought about Johann and Ken and how nice and quiet it must be just to have two people in an entire family. Even her nephew, Jeffy, had the ability to make her care. Or perhaps it was the fact that he was her nephew and she would care about him, no matter how many times he blew up her beach hat. She sighed deeply before she gained enough control over her anger at Janice to start speaking again.

"I really am glad that I have a caring family, but sometimes I wished I lived on a desert island. Now goodbye."

Gina hung up, disgusted with herself for her reaction to Janice's call, but even more disgusted with her family's continual overbearing reaction to everything she did in her life. She fluffed the pillows up behind her and tried to shake off the effects of the medicine she had taken the night before.

What was it? Wednesday? Maybe what she needed was to get out of town for a few days and just forget all about all of it.

Gina let Colleen out the back while she pulled on some sweats and rummaged around the kitchen for something to eat.

Yes, that was an idea. She'd drive to Chattanooga for the day and go to the world----class aquarium set beautifully on a little peninsula off the river. She would just call Andy and ask him to let Colleen out and give her dog a little one on one time, and feed her.

She'd even treat herself to a sit----down dinner, really treat herself, not the food court tacos she too often ate.

Having a plan in mind to fill up the day, Gina hurried

to take a shower and get dressed for her adventure.

Chapter Eight

Brrring, brrring, brrring!

The number rang again. No answer. Oh my God, where could she be? Ken hung up the phone and skimmed the phone book for the number for Grissom High School. It was 9:30 a.m. and he had no idea when she had a break or went to lunch.

"Grissom High School, may I help you?"

The voice on the other end of the phone sounded very young. Perhaps students worked in the office. Ken cleared his throat nervously.

"Yes. I wondered if Ms. Thompson was available to speakwith."

"Miss Thompson? You mean the science teacher?"
"Yes."

"Well, she called in sick. We had a sub first period."

"Thanks, thanks a lot." Ken hung up the phone immediately and called Gina's number. He hoped she wasn't really sick. Maybe she was just taking a day off. But he'd just spent the last thirty minutes trying to get her on her cell. He was sure that she wouldn't be home at 9:30 in the morning, so he hadn't bothered to call her house number, but he would now.

"You have reached…"

Ken's slammed the phone down. Man, where was she, where could she be? After a lot of soul---searching last night, he decided that it would a really smart move to pursue the relationship with Gina. No one could see the future. "The two hardest things to predict are the weather and the future." Someone clever had said that a long time ago. They were absolutely right. No one could predict the future. But sitting in his rented apartment on his rented couch wouldn't help him find his future; he had to go look for that himself. And the first thing he had to do to find his future was to find Gina Thompson and see how she felt about it.

Ken reached for the phone book, again, to look up

Andy's number. How many Andrew Thompsons could there be? And Andy had told him that he lived near him, so that would narrow it down even more.

There were only two Andrew Thompsons listed in the phone book and Ken decided by the address which one was the correct number. Ken punched in the number, and the very irritated voice of Andrew Thompson answered.

"What's going on, man?" asked Ken.

"As you might remember, I work swing shift so I can take afternoon classes. At this time, let me see, it's, what, let's see here, 9:39 a.m. I have been asleep for one hour and I've had three calls."

"Hey, I'm sorry, Andy, I'm trying to locate Gina. I didn't realize your shift had changed."

"Yeah, I usually do the seven to three and that way I can still get classes in, then a decent amount of sleep, and yes, I know where Gina is. She called me about twenty minutes ago and asked if I'd let Colleen out on my way to work. She's going to Chattanooga for the day to see the aquarium and get some dinner. And yes, she went alone. Janice called me as well. Janice just will not let up on her. Maybe she should have another kid and leave Gina alone. Now, I don't know when she left or even if she's left yet, I know from talking to my mom that my sister is pretty agitated about getting involved again."

"You mean with me?"

"No, man, with anyone. She is a mess when it comes to men and she has had more than her share of terrible relationships and I think she's just chicken."

Ken blew out a breath as he raked his hands through his hair. "Yeah, well, she's not the only one who is chicken."

"Listen, what is it with you two? I mean, get real. I have never met two people that were better suited to one another. And I am gleaning that information from not only being around you and your uncle, but also seeing the way Gina reacts each and every time one of us brings up your name. I mean, how many people could she talk to, or you talk to, about your work, the thing that encompasses your days, and can understand anything you say. But the two of you, it's like you speak the same language. And let's face it, you need more family, and she needs less. It's a match made... you know what I mean. Life is not getting any longer, my friend; it's way too short as it is. What if you just get on with it? You'll never know about one another if you keep avoiding each other. Think about it. I've got to go to bed now, Ken. Why don't you call me this afternoon say around 5 p.m.?"

"Thanks, man. I'll bring the beer next time."

"All right," said Andy and hung up the phone in the middle of a huge yawn. Without taking any time to think about it, Ken hurried out of his cubicle to his supervisor.

"I need the rest of the day off. It's personal."

His boss looked up in surprise. "Well, sure, Ken. Call me if you need tomorrow off, too."

"Sure, and thanks a lot, I appreciate it. I'll call and let you know about tomorrow, but I'll probably be in."

Ken went back to his cubicle and put in a call to Uncle Yo. He knew Uncle Yo would be at the senior center so he left a message on his machine. "I'll be back later tonight. I will call you as soon as I get in. Try not to burn down the house. Love you."

Ken looked in his wallet and decided he needed to take a stop at an ATM before he charged off to

Tennessee. He'd been to the aquarium; it was easy to find, right on a small peninsula jutting out into the Tennessee River. It even had its own exit off the interstate. He drove to the bank, gassed up the Jeep, and headed toward the interstate.

The lecture Andy had given him rolled through his mind over and over: "I've never seen two people better suited to one another... You both speak the same language... Life is just too short, get on with it."

Driving to Chattanooga, Tennessee, at 10:30 in the morning could most likely be defined as "getting on with it."

The trip was boring and uneventful and Ken finally pulled into the aquarium parking lot before lunch. He cruised around the lot first, looking for Gina's dark green car. Yes, there it was. Ken parked in the space beside her car and shut down the engine. He sat very still for a few minutes and let his brain run over the reasons he was here. Andy had said that life was short, what was he waiting for? What else did he say—get on with it and words to that effect.

"So, Ken, why are you here? Do you know why? Yes, I think you do. You're in love with Gina and you want to tell her so. There I go talking to myself again. As Gina says, 'I feel comfortable enough with myself to talk to myself.' So on with it, old man."

The wind blew like a gale off the Tennessee River, and Ken clutched the collar of his coat up to his neck. He hurried and paid his fee at the door.

Now, to find Gina.

Gina sat in contemplative silence in front of an exhibit that encompassed much of the ground floor, much as a connoisseur of fine art would sit in a gallery to admire the paintings. During the entire morning she had willed herself not to think about anything. She'd driven to Chattanooga in record time, only just obeying the speed limit.

She could see the headlines now:

This just in...teacher, from Grissom High School in Huntsville, stopped for speeding. Uses excuse of falling in love; the cop laughs.

Or maybe it would be: Gina Thompson, teacher at Grissom High School, was stopped for speeding: she said, 'I'm running away from my own feelings, and of course my family's incessant nagging.'

"Gross, Gina, you can't even make up a good headline anymore. What's becoming of your brain? Has it turned to mush?"

How did that old Cole Porter song go? "Falling in love again, da----da----da----da----da, da----da----da----da----da, can't help it." That was the problem, she couldn't remember the words. The last time she fell in love…

Her attention was drawn to a mottled, spotted, tiny crayfish the size of a fifty----cent piece, as it crawled by. Gina watched as he swam out of sight. Gosh, things were probably really easy if you were a fish, or a lobster, or something on the lower rungs of the evolutionary ladder. You just had to wait to hatch some babies and make sure a big fish didn't eat you.

Now, back to the question at hand, the last time she fell in love, when was it? Was it that guy Randy when she was an undergraduate? Maybe. How about her steady guy, Georgie, when she was in high school? Maybe. There hadn't been anyone since then that she had been seriously enamored of. No one. Maybe she didn't have enough experience to be in love.

Ken certainly fit the bill when it came to the kind of guy that she wanted to be in love with. He was terrific, magnificent, an all---- encompassing fifteen on a scale of one to ten. Why couldn't she just relax and let it happen?

Why? No experience; that was it. No experience. She'd been busy so much, and so consumed with her wonderful career, whatever that was, that she'd hadn't taken the time for important things like love. She'd had so many dates with Mr. Wrongs that she'd almost given up.

Still, she couldn't shake the dream of the evening before. The dream of the cold----hearted Ken as Sir Gregory had been so very real. The dream had shaken her to her core and along with that it had almost made her give up on Ken at 3:30 in the morning. That's why I'm here, she decided as she looked around. It was a great place to come and sit and just think.

A class filled with little kindergartners hurried into the room with their teacher and guide. They were pushing and giggling, holding hands, trying to make it up the ramp that led to the top of the aquarium, and generally having a magnificent time. Gina looked at their faces; they were so cute and trusting. So eager for everything that life was about to offer them. Why couldn't she be like that? Trusting? Bah humbug, 'my Aunt Fanny.'

Gina tore her gaze from the five----year----olds and wandered aimlessly up the ramp of the aquarium's main glassed----in series of tanks. Before she knew it, she was in front of the sharks. It was a long, deep area, so deep that it was difficult to see the bottom of the tank. Yard after yard of deadly----looking, and in some cases, huge, prehistoric fish swam by, completely ignoring her. Gina cocked her head as she looked at the hammerhead that swam by.

"Hmm, he looks a little like my boss. And that nurse shark over there, reminds me of...Janice of course."

She still couldn't fathom why Janice had had the audacity to call her this morning and ask her where she was. Of course she had the audacity, and Janice's audacity was getting worse by the day. What if she'd been lying in bed with Ken? What if Ken gave her a look like Sir Gregory from her dream had?

"Life cannot be so out of control and complicated that you can't even live it, Thompson."

Gina stood with her nose practically pressed to the glass when a familiar shape reflected in the tank caught her eye. She stood back, staring at the image of Ken standing directly behind her. Gina shook her head, trying to dislodge the image.

"You're losing it, girl. Now you're seeing things," she said to herself.

"Would you like to get some lunch?" the voice of the reflection said.

Gina stuck her finger in her ear and waggled it back and forth. Was she hearing a buzzing or had she heard a real voice?

"Gina, do you want to get some lunch?" the voice said again.

Gina turned slowly and Sir Gregory, uh, Ken, stood smiling down at her.

"Hi, do you come here often?" he asked.

"I think I need to sit down. It must be lack of sleep, or just my brain has finally turned to mush, but you look like the guy that I'm falling in l..."

"The guy that you're falling in what with?"

Gina shook her head again. She took a deep breath, striving for complete control of herself. She looked up into those violet----blue eyes and took another deep breath, the fog finally lifting so that she could think.

"Ken, what're you doing here?" "I came to see you, of course."

Gina cocked an eyebrow at him. "You mean the fish hold no special interest for you?"

"No," said Ken as he reached out and took her hand in his, pulling her closer to him. "But you do. I was worried about you today."

Worried, that word... worried. How many times had she heard that word even in the space of one morning? First, her idiotic, lame----brained family, and now... Did everyone in the world think she was a complete nincompoop and could not take care of herself? Gina pulled away and frowned at Ken.

"Why is everyone in the whole bloody world is worried about me? Do I really appear to be so completely incompetent that I am incapable of taking care of myself?"

Women.

Ken tried hard not to roll his eyes. He had pondered a decision dealing with why he was there for a very long time sitting in his car. Why was he there? Was he in Chattanooga because he loved Gina and wanted to tell her so, or was he here because he needed to find out how he first felt about her?

He'd searched the aquarium for almost a half hour, running into and then surrounded by a class of little urchins. He'd managed to circumnavigate three more classes of students of various sizes before he had finally seen Gina at the shark exhibit. She was standing very still, her shoulders hunched forward, talking to herself. Again. He'd heard something about the hammerhead looking like the principle of Grissom High, and then she'd muttered something about her big sister, Janice. She looked so forlorn, so alone, so miserable. The last time he'd seen her she'd been so happy and animated. What had happened?

"Do you want to go to lunch?" he'd said, and she'd

just stood there. Then she mumbled something about Sir Gregory. And now, she looked as though she wanted him to get lost. What was going on?

"Gina, what's the matter? And, by the way, I'm here to see you. And, I do not think you are a nincompoop. I think you're the smartest person I know. You could've gone to MIT and been an astrophysics engineer or a cosmologist if you'd wanted to. I don't know what was stopping you. Now, why do you look so depressed? It's not like you to be so self----critical."

Gina struggled against the dream that had shattered her good night's sleep and her resolve to get involved with Ken. Maybe, if her family would stay out of her life...no, she just couldn't blame this one on her family. It wasn't really her bad dream that was upsetting her, even though that had been the beginning of this heavy layer of depression that was pushing down on her. She sat heavily on a nearby bench.

The thought struck her squarely in the chest and took all of the breath from her, like a fall from a high ladder. Her family had always tried to get her fixed up. They'd always been matchmaking, worrying her to death about why she wasn't married. And now here they were again, pushing Ken on her and she just wasn't ready. No sirree, she just wasn't ready. What if he treated her like all of the others had? That was her problem; it wasn't because of her family or Ken.

She looked at Ken squarely. He was so terrific, and he even thought she was smart. Hadn't he just told her that she could've gone to MIT? She'd never even considered going to any school but Alabama or Georgia Tech. And why hadn't she? What was it about her self----esteem that had kept her from even considering something else?

She was thinking small again. She was not pushing herself forward with her schooling or with Ken. Maybe all this time she thought her family were the ones who were doing all of pushing. Oh, this self----reproach is ridiculous. She supposed she could blame her bad dreams on all of the self----retrospect. She turned and looked at Ken. Again. He was so great to come all the way to Chattanooga and see her. He obviously felt something for her that he was ready to explore. Why couldn't she just let it happen? He had on that navy sweater again. He was so very handsome, and such a good person inside and out. Gina's good manners began to overrule her fuddled brain.

"Ken, you are so sweet to come all this way. How did you find out where I was?"

"I called the school, you weren't there. I thought that maybe you were sick so I worried and called you at home, but there was no answer. Then I called Andy." Ken sat next to her and reached for her hand. He looked down for a moment and sketched his thumb over her knuckles, feeling the dewy softness of her skin. He looked up and tried for a big smile. "Of course, I was the third of fourth call he'd had since getting off the graveyard shift. Your family really cares about you. They really love you, it's so clear how they feel. It irritates you so much that they are always hanging around, and I can't understand why. Can you imagine if you only had a grouchy old uncle like I have?"

"Yes, it would be sheer heaven."

"No, it wouldn't be, Gina," said Ken. He gazed at her hand for a long moment, feeling the warmth and silkiness of her skin. He looked up at her and turned her chin toward him so that she would look at him. "You'd be miserable. And that's why I'm here."

"I don't get it?"

"I want to be a part of that huge network of people that cares about you. I want you to care about me too."

"Ken, I do care very much for you. Very much, I'm just…" "Are you chicken?"

"Yeah, that's it."

"I don't know what's going to happen a year from now, a day from now, who knows that?"

Gina worked up a little smile as she shrugged her shoulders. "Should we call the psychic network?"

Ken laughed so loud people turned and stared. As he wiped the tears from his eyes, he turned to Gina and gave her a solid hug. He reached for her hand again and, leaning forward, gave her a peck on the cheek.

"I don't think so. Let's go out to that restaurant on the boardwalk and eat lunch. If you want to eat something else today, I'll take you there."

"Thanks, Ken, as usual, you are a real gentleman. Can

I ask you something?"

"Shoot."

"Tell me about the picture in your bedroom."

Ken closed his eyes in concentration for a moment, trying to remember which picture she was talking about. He had several on his walls, some of his mother's German birthplace, some of his parents, and then he remembered the painting that he'd had made at a Renaissance fair last year.

"You mean the painting of the knight?" "Yes, that's the one."

"That's me," he said quizzically. He couldn't imagine what she was driving at. What had that picture to do with anything? Why had she picked that picture out to obsess about, even a little?

Gina gave a little laugh, and pulled her hand away from Ken's. "No kidding."

"I went to a Renaissance fair in Birmingham last year. Let's go this year and we'll have one of you painted in a medieval costume."

"Yeah, like Lady Katherine De'Venchie," Gina

muttered. "Who?"

"Oh, never mind. I've been having some bad dreams lately. I guess they have me pretty shaken. That and the meddling of my overbearing family."

That remark Ken would leave alone. The last thing he needed was to get into the middle of some broo-
---ha----ha between Gina and her family. He would be Switzerland, always neutral. That is until they were actually married; then he'd come to Gina's rescue every time. "Let's go get some lunch, and we'll shelve this for a while. If you want to talk after you feel better, then we'll do it."

"Okay, I guess. Isn't there a cafeteria downstairs?"
"No, we'll have to go out to the boardwalk."

Ken and Gina circumvented several more classes of children on their way outside. In the restaurant, there was lots of noise from happy kids, adults calling loudly over the laughing, and the clatter of dishes and cutlery.

Gina looked at the assortment of lunchtime foods offered, not thrilled by any of them. The sausage biscuit she'd eaten at a fast food drive----in had tasted like sawdust and unfortunately continued to do so.

She got a glass of soda and a cellophane----wrapped ham sandwich. The late night of reading, and dreaming, the hour and a half drive, and the taco last night were decidedly not agreeing with her. She started to feel as green as her ski jacket.

Ken looked up at Gina. She looked really awful. Anxiety edged every frown line on her green----tinged face. Could it be him that she was sick of?

He'd come a long way because he wanted her to know how he felt about her. He'd decided that he was not going to drag his feet any longer and just get on with it, as Andy had said. When he hadn't been able to find her this morning, his own anxiety had hit him like a ton of bricks. He wanted this woman in the worst way. Not just her body, although that would be extremely nice, but her personality, her laughing at his drier----than----dust jokes. Everything about her made him feel good and alive. As Andy had said, they spoke the same language. She made him feel good and real and he didn't know how long it been since he felt that way. He liked the person he was when he was around her. The world of his work had just about taken over his life. He'd fallen into a routine of going to work, seeing Uncle Yo, going to the gym, and playing with computers.

Was that living? No, it was more like purgatory. Gina made him think about really living again. Not just the paralyzing everyday routine that could be almost impossible to break out of. He hoped he could make her feel the same way. She looked as green as her jacket, and her head was tucked down so far he could see only the very top of it.

"You look sick."

"I am sick. Redheads look green when they get sick." "Do you want an antacid or something?"

"No, I'll just sip on the soda."

A long silence stretched out encompassing their little table. They were like an island amidst the hustle and bustle of the lunch café. Ken didn't talk, he just sat and every once in a while he'd take a bite of his salad or drink a sip of his coffee. He was ever conscious of Gina and her downcast head.

Gina stared down at her soda, struggling with the turmoil in her heart and the awful way her body was feeling. She just couldn't love him. What if he hurt her? What if her family drove her to a lunatic asylum? And right now that was a distinct possibility, a charming, if not plausible thought.

Things were sure easier in the old days. You just went to the castle with your knight, brought up the children, managed the gardens and the servants, and made sure the Lord of the keep was satisfied with his supper and with you.

The painting in Ken's bedroom still unnerved her. It looked too much like the imagined knight of her daydreams; the whole scenario was just too weird for words. Gina sighed deeply and felt the fog lift a little from her head.

Should she keep up this pretense of aloofness? She really thought he was so wonderful. The man drove all the way to Chattanooga to see you for crying out loud. Gina peeked at him from under her lashes, and suddenly another headline flashed through her mind:

This just in…man proposes to teacher in front of shark tank: details coming up after the break.

Good grief. Gina, get a grip.

Gina's head came up just a tiny bit, and Ken reached over and squeezed her hand.

"Can you tell me why you're so unhappy?"

"No, I don't know if I can put it into words. I guess the bottom line is, I'm starting to care about you too much, and it scares the life out of me. I've never met anyone that was so good and kind and I guess I'm so used to dealing with the scum of the earth that I don't know how to act. And my family doesn't help any." Gina looked up then, and stared blatantly at Ken.

"They push so hard that I just want to push back. Do you know what I mean? The 'I'm not gonna do what you tell me, even if it's good for me, because you told me to' syndrome."

"I know exactly how you feel. Uncle Yo has been pushing too hard for a very long time. Sometimes, I just hang up on him, because he drives me crazy."

Gina looked up again and tried to smile. Complications. That's what this was, complications. She would have to deal with it, but she would have to deal with it after she'd had some sleep. More important, she'd turn off her cell and unplug her landline. She looked back down at the wrapped ham sandwich and her tummy did a little flip----flop. She made an immediate decision. "Ken, I'm going to go home and veg out with an old movie. Sometimes, when my mind is otherwise engaged, I can talk to myself sensibly. It's not that I don't care for you, because I do. I just can't think about it right now. My head is giving me a fit and I'm going to go home and lie down."

Gina got up from her chair, and without looking at Ken walked out of the restaurant and headed to the parking lot.

Distance. That was what she needed right now. Distance.

Ken watched Gina's retreating back as she disappeared from view. What on earth had just transpired? She was messed up about something. A dream, getting involved with him, she told him that she really cared for him. She just wasn't ready, she just wasn't.

THIS JUST IN

Chapter Nine

Gina turned the key in the lock and pushed herself through to the kitchen. Colleen made a happy yelp and gave her a kiss. The trip had been agonizingly slow, and several times she'd pulled off into a rest area and let her head fall back against the seat until the fog in her mind had lifted.

The cold seeping into the car had always jarred her awake and she'd driven a little further. It was after three o'clock when she finally made it up the mountain to her house.

"Hey, girl, did you have a good day? Go on outside for a while."

Gina went to the medicine cabinet and fixed an antacid. She held her nose, but still shivered after she'd got it down. She drank a quick glass of soda to wash the taste away. She hung up her coat and then

211

let Colleen in, shivering again as the wind whipped around the door. Colleen jogged back in the kitchen and flopped unceremoniously on to the kitchen floor, her tongue lolling out of her mouth. Gina wondered about how easy it would be to be a dog. She pushed herself off the edge of the counter and made herself eat a bowl of oatmeal and a banana.

She curled onto the couch with an afghan over her knees, the heater lit, and began watching the first movie she turned to that was in black and white.

No, it was one of those film noir stories from the `50s. Yuck. She looked through her cache of films and found an old Hepburn/Tracy movie. It was the one about the high class writer who married a sports reporter. That one was great, although it was a little more serious than she wanted right now.

The movie played through the scene where Tracy got disgusted with Hepburn. She'd left their Greek war orphan they'd temporarily adopted in the hands of the doorman. It always made Gina uncomfortable to hear Hepburn getting chewed out, even when she deserved to get chewed out.

Gina sat in a stupor as the story, the story she knew

so well, played out in front of her. She was great at not thinking about things when she wanted to. But watching Tracy love Hepburn so unconditionally made her think of Ken. She just wondered. Was Ken on the way to loving her unconditionally? And consequently, was she on the way to that unconditional love as well? Life was not a fairytale, life was not a fantasy, but as Tammy said, "You have to live life, not crawl in a hole and pull it in after you." She sighed deeply, and Colleen pulled her head up, whining a little in the back of her throat. The poor dog was like a sponge to any and all of Gina's emotions.

The movie was almost at an end when Gina heard the kitchen door open. Colleen didn't move from her spot on the rug, but just half----heartedly beat her tail with a thump, thump, thump. Gina knew it was Andy.

"Hi."

"What are you doing here? I thought you were in Chattanooga with Ken."

Gina heaved a big sigh, and with a flourish and much ceremony clicked off the TV. She sat quietly on the couch for a moment staring at the blank screen, feeling, but not seeing Andy with his hands on his hips in the kitchen doorway. Her family!

They could be…

"Well, I guess I left early." "How come?"

"I didn't feel good." "You didn't feel good?"

"That's right," said Gina. She turned to give Andy a level look. "See, I'm sick to death of my family," she said sarcastically.

"Gina, when are you going to get a grip? Ken would love it if he had a family who cared about him the way we care about you. So what gives? You want to wave a magic wand and have everyone disappear?"

"Gosh," said Gina as she threw the afghan off her knees, and stood quickly with her hands braced on her hips. "That's not a bad idea." She knew they looked like bookends, both standing with their hands on their hips, so she sat back down with another flourish, held the remote like it was a magic wand, and clicked it on.

"I thought you really cared for Ken. Do you or don't you?" Gina clicked the set off again and turned to face Andy. "Yes,

yes, I love him, is that what you want to hear?" she said angrily. She sat back in a slump with her arms folded across her chest. She glanced down at Colleen. The poor dog looked completely confused. She and Andy rarely fought. But now she was ready, she was ready for a rip roaring, knockdown and drag out fight to the finish. And the problem was she didn't even know why.

Andy turned a blind eye to her fit of temper. "Well, now we're getting somewhere. Did you tell him?"

"No, I left." "You left?"

"Well, I started to get a little green and I knew that I was botching it up because I couldn't even look at him...so, I left. I think I told him that I wasn't ready. It's all a foggy memory, I guess I'm not sure what I said and I hope it wasn't so bad he'll never speak to me again." Gina sat back on the couch and draped her arm over her eyes. Andy could look right inside her. No one else in the world could, but he could.

Andy shook his head, paced, stopped, and shook his head again. He sat on the couch next to Gina, put his arm around her, and hugged her fiercely. "What are you waiting for? Life is awfully short... remember

215

when our cousin Jim died last year and he was our age, and we had a really serious talk about getting on with our lives? Don't you know how old you are?"

"Well, duh. What am I, two minutes younger than you?" Gina said. She sighed then turned and hugged Andy back.

He was the best brother, the best. She closed her eyes and thought about what he'd just said. "Don't you know how old you are...Life is short...Remember when our cousin Jim died and we talked?"

"You have to decide in your own mind why you can't decide. What is holding you back? Ken is not going to wait forever for you, and he shouldn't have to. Having to work graveyard shift and swing shift helps a person see what their priorities are. As I said, and I hate to nag, life is indeed very short. Take advantage of all the good things that are happening to you. And get on with it. Those were the very words I told Ken this morning." Andy put his head back and chucked Gina under the chin to make sure she was listening. "I've never met anyone that I'd rather have as my brother----in----law." Andy rose from the couch and grabbed his jacket. "Please think about it. Don't let this opportunity slip by without at least giving the guy a chance."

Andy dug into his pockets and slipped on his gloves. He made his way to the kitchen door, and gave Colleen a rub behind the ears before he reached for the doorknob. "Oh, by the way, a bad storm is moving in. I heard a report on the radio on the way over here. I have a feeling we'll be at work, make a showing, and then they'll send us home. Do you have enough kerosene, dog food, milk, and those kinds of things?"

"Oh, brother," said Gina grabbing for her coat and gloves and heading for the door with Andy. "That's all we need is another ice storm."

"It's still just six. Go on out and stock up now before everybody and their brother cleans out the stores." Andy reached down and kissed Gina on the cheek. He looked into her eyes and made sure she was looking back before he spoke. "I want you to be happy. Don't get in the way of your own happiness."

Gina ruffled Andy's hair and kissed him back. They reached for the doorknob at the same exact second and laughed.

"I'll take your advice and run to the store. And I

promise I will think about what you've said about Ken...and life being so short. I'll call you later about what I've come up with. You and Rachel come on over if you lose your heat." She looked at her brother for just a second and then kissed him again." I love you, Andy."

"I love you too, Gina. Don't get in the way of yourself."

"I'll give it my best shot."

Ken stood in the center of his living room rug watching the TV weatherman forecast doom. Another ice storm was on its way for the city and outlying areas of Huntsville. He made his way to his kitchen and quickly scanned his refrigerator and shelves, deciding that he had enough stores to last for a few days. His jeep was gassed up, and the four----wheel drive could make it through anything old Mother Nature threw at him. He could even climb Monte Sano Mountain and get to Gina if he chose to. That is, if she would let him. Ken slammed the refrigerator door with a curse.

Why? Why when everything was moving along so well did she have to get cold feet? He'd have time to sort it all out now if he was going to be iced in with Uncle Yo for a few days. Uncle Yo! He'd better make sure his uncle was all right and that there was enough wood for the fireplace and stores in the kitchen.

Ken quickly picked up the phone and speed dialed his uncle. "Uncle Yo?"

"Oh, hello, my boy. And has that cat of yours got enough kitty litter to ride out the storm?"

"So, you've heard the news."

"Ah, yes. But do not worry, my boy. I have just gone to the grocery, and bought coffee and things to eat. I went to the German bakery and bought a half of a Schwarze Wald Kuchen. I even have a little brandy and some schnapps in case it gets really cold."

"Do you have enough wood inside?"

"Ah, yes, my boy. I have carried the wood in all day and I have filled the garage with it. I have called my lady friend and her daughter will bring her here to my house tonight so she will have a nice warm place to stay. Now, how is Gina? Such a lovely girl."

"She's fine, Uncle Yo. I saw her today, and Andy called and told me he'd check on her before he went to work," said Ken, not able to keep the exasperation from leaking through the phone. Uncle Yo would have to bring up Gina! Ken hoped he could avoid the many uncomfortable questions Uncle Yo could put to him.

"That is very good, my boy. She will be stuck but good in her little mountain house with no way to get off if the ice comes down too bad. I am glad you have that jeep of yours. And I am glad you took the time to put on the tire chains. It will carry you to Gina's in no time. If she needs a rescue, that is."

Ken tried to stop the next sigh from coming out and giving Uncle Yo any more ammunition, but Uncle Yo caught that sigh and chortled with glee. "You will do the right thing, my boy. I brought you up and you know what to do. Now tus. Take extra good care of yourself and call me tomorrow, but not too early, eh?"

Ken sighed again as he hung up the phone and went into his bedroom. Maybe he'd lie down and take a little nap, just in case Uncle Yo called him in the middle of the night to go get his "lady friend."

Ken opened the top drawer of his dresser and pulled out a fleece----lined sweater. The sweater was usually too hot to wear any place outside of Austria, but he just knew the electricity would go off and he might as well be warm.

As he closed his door, his eye was drawn to the picture he'd had painted of himself at the Renaissance fair last year. The painting had rattled Gina and he wondered why. Why had seeing him as the knight in his suit of armor upset her so much? And more importantly, had he done anything to make her pull from him now?

He'd nap now so if Uncle Yo needed him in the middle of the night, he'd be awake and sharp. Perhaps if he took a nap, he could get his head to screw on straight when he tried to untangle his thoughts about Gina.

"So, my dear Janice, I have just talked to Ken and he tells me that he has seen Gina today. Do you think that if the storm hits, maybe they will be forced to be together? Maybe all our plans will finally come about with the help of Mother Nature."

"Johann, that's not the half of it. Andy tells me that she took the day off and went to Chattanooga and Ken followed her there."

"What? Why, that is wonderful. Wahoo! Maybe we're going to get some results."

"Yes, but that's not all. Andy told me that Gina went back home without Ken. And Andy thinks Gina has cold feet. We'll no doubt need to find something else to force them into a situation to be together. Gina is very upset with everyone in the family. She thinks we're pushing her too hard."

"Well, perhaps the storm will aid us." "How?"

"Why certainly, what we can't accomplish, maybe Old Man Winter will. One lives on a mountain, and can't get off and has a heater that the weather can't affect. The other can get up the mountain, but has heat that will shut off by the time the first snowflake falls. I think our problems will be over in a few days. Now, how will we get these two stubborn people to reach out when they are in need?"

"I've got a few ideas, why don't you leave that to

me?"

"Wunderbar! I will call you if I have any news." "I'll talk to you soon, Johann."

Gina hurried to the nearest convenience store and gas station that sold kerosene. Andy was right, Huntsville had snow/ice fever, and everyone was getting stocked up. The TV set braced in the corner of the little store was tuned into her favorite weatherman.

"And as you can see," he said to the camera. "The front is moving in rapidly and I predict that it will leave several inches of snow on the Tennessee Valley. The problem will be, however, that the temperatures will plummet and we will experience below zero temperatures for perhaps several days."

A groan went up from the people gathered around the TV set in the little store.

"My goodness," said one man. "I hope my pipes will hold up."

"Me too," said another. "I'm sure glad I had that extra antifreeze put in the other day."

Gina looked around her sadly. Even though it usually snowed once or twice a season in Huntsville, no one was prepared for the brutally cold temperatures. The houses were not built for it. Neither were the sidewalks or the roads. The really cold temperatures just didn't happen often enough for it to be a problem. She quickly made her purchases, including another gallon of kerosene, and left the store. It was seven o'clock and the first flakes had begun to fall.

Gina drove inside her garage and shut the door. Thoughts of Ken crashed around her like a ton of bricks. She shook her head as she put away her purchases, and held the door for Colleen to go out.

"Go on, girl, you won't be happy putting your feet in the cold snow, so do whatever you need to do now and get it over with." Colleen whimpered a little as she cocked her head but went out. Gina catalogued her supplies. She had a gallon and a half of kerosene, a half----gallon of milk, bread, hot dogs, food for Colleen, teabags, sugar, coffee, and even a half dozen cans of her favorite curly noodle lasagna. She was definitely set for a few days at least. Continuing with her inspection, Gina started all the taps dripping and went to the garage to make sure the outside water was turned off at the source. Gina fervently hoped the pipes in her house could stand it.

Maybe she'd come up with a solution to her nagging problems if she were forced to stay in her little house for several days. She wouldn't have school tomorrow, of that she was sure. One of the benefits of living on the mountain, if you could call it that, was staying home when the ice got too bad. The sand trucks had a lot to do to bring the major thoroughfares up to snuff before they could tackle Monte Sano Mountain.

"Come on, girl," called Gina to Colleen. The snow had started to come down in buckets and Colleen shook the wet chunks off her coat as she came to the door. Gina bent down and brushed the remaining clumps of snow from Colleen's back and then mopped up the mess with paper towels.

She'd done all she could do at the moment. She made herself some soup and carried it into the living room to turn on the news. She'd watch her weatherman for a while and then turn her movie back on.

After the movie, she'd think about Ken and start to decide what to do.

THIS JUST IN

Chapter Ten

The snow came down in big fat flakes and Gina turned on her floodlights and watched for a while as the flakes did their beautiful dance, swirling, ducking, and twirling. It was gorgeous, especially so if the event came only once or twice a year. And it was especially lovely if you didn't have to drive anyplace. There were crazy people who didn't know how to drive in snow and ice, but somehow thought they did. Needing to get on the roads and wanting to get on the roads were decidedly two different things. And she didn't have to do either right now.

Gina had checked in with her family, grudgingly. Janice was quite contrite, and had apologized at least three times for disturbing her that day and for setting her up with a complete loser last Friday night. Gina decided that Janice would just need to suffer a little longer, and said nothing to her, but bye as she hung up the phone.

She hadn't called Ken as yet. It was just too soon. She'd just left him a few hours before, and he was most likely furious with her. Furious. She guessed she couldn't blame him; he'd come all the way to Chattanooga to be serious about her and she said she wasn't ready. But after Andy's lecture, which she taken quite to heart, it surprised her that she was in fact, at least for the last thirty seconds, ready to make a decision about a life with Ken. She felt her will vacillate from one option to the next about the problem, about the decision, so maybe she wasn't ready to fall.

It was the dreams, the dreams that had messed up her head temporarily and sent her screaming over the edge. They were dreams, just dreams.

Gina thought about the way her mind always went into TV reporter mode. She'd been doing that for as long as she could remember. The internal journalist way of thinking was certainly related to the daydreams, and the dreams. Perhaps tonight she would read her new astronomy journal that had come in the mail. It might be a good idea to put the medieval and the other romances down for a while until she could get her head on straight.

Gina turned off the floodlights and went to the TV to check on the latest. The front had arrived and stalled over the Tennessee Valley. The temperature was already seventeen degrees and falling.

Gina logged into her e----mail; maybe she'd write to Ken instead of calling. That was always a great avoidance tactic.

Dear Ken,

Thanks for coming to the aquarium today.

I know I acted like a dork but other than bad dreams and lack of sleep, I have no excuse.

Andy came to see me before he went on shift. After our talk I am convinced that he could get work as one of the ancient sages we used to read about in our history books. Yes, he talked to me too. We can get together after the storm if you want to and talk all this out.

I'd like that. I think we need to.

Gina

"Wow, Gina could you be any more redundant?" Gina deleted the e----mail and then absently rubbed Colleen under the chin. She'd have to fix this mess she'd gotten herself into. Either she loved him and wanted him in her life or she didn't.

She knew she loved him, but what about all the rest of it? Could she love the guy forever? She thought for just a second, then she thought again, then she thought some more.

Yes, she could love him without reservation, Gina knew she absolutely could. Absolutely. She could see the headlines now:

This just in…Teacher finally decides she's had enough of the single life. Plans to marry engineer. More after the break.

"Gina, get a grip." With that bit of daydreaming out of the way, Gina turned on her movie and settled down to watch and wait. Maybe she was waiting to see how bad the storm would become. In her heart, she knew she waited for Ken. Waited to see what was going to happen.

Ken woke up to the howling wind. The wind whistled and churned around his windows and blew things against the side of the apartment building. He reached his hand over to switch on the lights. The electricity was decidedly out.

He shivered as he fumbled for the flashlight he kept in his bedside drawer. Groping for the hallway, he found the thermostat on the wall. It read fifty---eight degrees and the temperature was going to fall even further. He checked his watch, noting that it was ten p.m. already. He'd call Uncle Yo and make sure that he was all right.

"Uncle Yo," he said none too clearly because his teeth were chattering.

"Yes, are you without heat? I can tell because your teeth are knocking together. Is that cat of yours not sitting on your feet?"

"Not at the moment. Are you all right?"

"Yes, now I'm sorry I can't invite you over, but my lady friend is here. Why don't you go over to Gina's? She has the heater."

"No, that's okay. I'll just ride it out." Ken hung up the

phone after a fast goodbye left him feeling depressed and strangely rejected. Could he call Gina? Not now. Maybe sometime, but not now. Even if he stayed warm enough, there was no way to make food or coffee.

There was no need for coffee or food right now, he supposed. Ken went to the closet and found his mother's feather bed that he kept wrapped in a big plastic bag. Outside, the storm raged. Ken stared into the inky blackness trying very hard not to think at all. He finally fell asleep.

•••◐●◑•••

"Gina? It's Janice."

"Yeah, do you realize what time it is?"

"Yes, it's near midnight. I was calling to see if you were warm enough."

"Yes, I'm warm enough and I can even heat soup and coffee.

Ah, my little heater. It certainly is a handy thing. "

"That's great. The reason I'm calling is I just heard from Andy. They sent them home early, and he's gone over to Rachel's because she has a fireplace. But Ken is without any power at all. Why don't you call him? The poor guy's probably got frostbite by now."

"Janice, you are so terribly transparent."

"The poor guy's probably freezing and here you are thinking everyone is pushing you. And nobody is. Nobody. Look, if you don't want to rescue the guy, it will be on your conscience, not mine. I could invite him here, but your place is at least 20 miles closer."

"Point taken. Now, I want you to raise your right hand." "Huh?"

"Do it."

"Okay, my right hand is raised."

"Repeat after me, I do solemnly swear... " "Gina!"

"Do it! 'I do solemnly swear that I will leave my little sister's life alone, even if her romance with Ken does not work out.' Now say it, because if you don't, you and I are going to be at odds for a very long time. You don't want Mom to start crying again like she did last Christmas do you?"

"Okay, okay, I swear it. I really do, Gina. I know I

push too hard. I will, as of this moment, leave you alone. So solemnly sworn."

"Now, if it starts to look like the juice will be off for a long time, I'll call Ken. I promise I won't let him suffer frostbite."

"Good. I love you, Gina."

"I love you too, bye. I'll call tomorrow."

Gina tuned into her AM station on her battery---
-operated radio and listened to the latest updates on the storm. It was a bad one. The ice and snow were still coming down and the wind chill factor was now at fifteen degrees below zero. Not too bad if you're living in the Yukon, but down right insane if you're in the Heart of Dixie.

Gina decided she wouldn't call Ken, not until the storm let up and he could see more than two feet in front of his face. She didn't want him to risk coming up the mountain. Well, after all, he was a big boy. She supposed he could decide whether or not he could make it. Gina reached for the phone, but before she could dial, she slammed down the receiver. Then she picked it up again and punched in Ken's number. The number rang once, twice.

"Hello, Uncle Yo?" murmured a sleepy voice on the other end of the phone. "Hello, hello, is anyone there?"

Gina held the receiver away from her for another split second, deciding whether she should hang up or speak up. She waited a split second more, pondering at her indecision.

"Hello?"

"Ken, it's Gina." "Are you okay?"

Wow, the first thing he asked was if she okay. Gina started getting a little teary----eyedand she realized with abundant clarity just how special Ken was.

"Yes, I'm fine." Gina took a big breath and plunged in before she could change her mind. It was the right thing to do. And more importantly, it was what she wanted to do, because she wanted Ken. "I have a heat source and you don't. If you want to drive up here and stay with me, I'd like that."

Ken let out a big breath. "Is it still snowing?" "Yes, it's coming down in buckets."

"Well, I'm warm right now. I pulled my mother's feather bed out of the storage closet. I'll be starved when tomorrow finally gets here, so I'll make it up the mountain when the sun comes up. Can you cook on the heater?"

Gina sighed inwardly. Now that she'd made up her mind, she was loath to wait even an extra minute, an extra minute without him. But she would put no pressure on him. She knew what pressure felt like, because she had Janice's example to try not to follow.

"Yes, I've got it all worked out: soup, hot dogs, chili, even a little steak, coffee. You know, necessity is the mother of invention. But if you do come, please be very careful, I want you to get here in one piece. And Ken, there are things to talk about, things to say."

A thousand thoughts ran through Ken's mind, but the one that was at the forefront was that she cared about him, she wanted him to get there, that "there were things to talk about, things to say." He grinned.

"I will. I have lots to be careful for now."

Gina felt the heat rush to her cheeks as she hung up the phone. He had lots to be careful for now. He meant her, she was why he needed to be careful. She just knew he meant her. He wanted her and she wanted him, this was too good, too good to be true, and for once she knew that it really was.

She snuggled down into her comforter and fell asleep. She dreamed of knights in golden castles and ladies in long flowing gowns. The sun glinted off the castle's long spires, as flags fluttered in a gentle breeze.

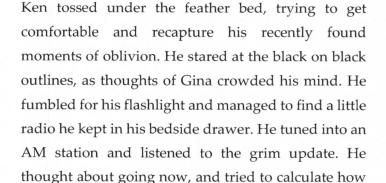

Ken tossed under the feather bed, trying to get comfortable and recapture his recently found moments of oblivion. He stared at the black on black outlines, as thoughts of Gina crowded his mind. He fumbled for his flashlight and managed to find a little radio he kept in his bedside drawer. He tuned into an AM station and listened to the grim update. He thought about going now, and tried to calculate how safe it would be and how much risk he would take.

He listened for a while, comforted to feel Butch sleeping across his feet. He was surprised the cranky old cat hadn't crawled under the feather bed with him.

Thinking of his feather bed made him think of Gina,

and thinking of Gina spurred him on to do something rash, something he wouldn't have even contemplated a few weeks before. Ken rammed his feet into his boots, put on his goose down parka and gloves, a knitted cap, and ran out to start the jeep. The wind tore at his cheeks, making his eyes tear fiercely so that he could hardly see. He wiped at the tears as he scraped as much snow as he could off the windshield He hoped that the car's heater and special windshield solution would do the rest.

Ken ran back into the apartment, and with the aid of the wavering beam of the flashlight, he grabbed essentials and stuffed them into his duffel, grabbed the cantankerous yowling Butch and put him into his carrying case, and carried them to the car. He retraced his steps and got some additional supplies and Butch's cat box and locked up the apartment.

The ice and wind blew at his face with a ferocity that took his breath away. He struggled to make his way to the car, but the violent wind picked up considerably and blew against him, pushing him back toward the apartments. Within seconds, bits of ice crystals plastered down his eyelids and crusted his eyebrows.

He roughly scoured his gloved hand across his face so that he could see. He managed to pull the door open, and deposited the extra items in the back. Butch sat in the right front seat in his carrier. The poor cat was cold and cantankerous and growled as Ken slammed the jeep's door shut. The cat put up an awful yowl, so loud that it almost drowned out the sound of the wind.

———————————•◦●◯●◦•———————————

Gina dreamed. She wasn't awake, but she wasn't asleep either. Her consciousness and subconscious all ran together in a great muddy stream. Potent dreams made her exhaustion all the more fretful. Even asleep, she had a conscious awareness of the fatigue that plagued her and crept into every joint. She turned over, sighed, yawned, and drifted back into a semi---sleep, and dreamed again of knights.

The knights were jousting in a dusty, sunny field. The knight in the burnished black armor, helm on, rode with great self---- confidence into the center of the field. He saluted the king and queen of the joust and slowly rode to the field of honor. The shields of all the knights hung from long poles under the king's

239

pavilion. With utter defiance, he slammed his lance against each of the shields. Gina heard her name called, the knight turned and looked right at her. Gina heard her name called again.

"What?"

Gina scrubbed at her eyes with the heels of her hands, and she slowly realized that someone was banging on the front door, and it wasn't the wind. Colleen frantically tried to lick her awake, making sharp little barks.

Gina sat up and swung her legs over the edge of the couch and stumbled in the dark to the front door. Colleen gave one sharp bark and looked at her expectantly. She pushed aside the curtain but could see nothing in the dark.

"Who is it?"

"Gina, it's me. I'm freezing out here." "Ken?"

Gina hurried to open the door and Ken staggered in with a cat carrier, litter box, and a duffel bag all hanging from his arms.

"Hold the door open. I've got to get him inside quick. And me too, I guess."

Gina held open the door as Ken managed to get everything inside. She was shivering by the time she managed to get the door closed pushing hard against the howling, bitter wind. Ken braced himself against the closed door, breathing heavily.

"It's dark in here."

"Well, it comes with the power being out. Just a minute, I think I can find the lantern. Don't move, you'll trip."

Gina felt around the end of the couch, located the lantern, and turned it on. The light bathed the room in a harsh glare and Ken and Gina both shielded their eyes.

Colleen sniffed at Ken and beat her tail against the rug happily. She gave the cat carrier a good sniff, and backed off quickly as Butch's low growl came from the depths of the carrier.

"Hey, Butch, mind your manners."

"I'll put him in the back room until they get used to each other," said Gina taking the carrier from Ken. "Why don't you go sit down before you fall down."

Gina moved down the darkened hall with Butch

growling and hissing all the way. Ken staggered to the couch and sat heavily as Colleen put her head between his knees and thumped her tail against the floor. The room was warm, so much warmer than the jeep. His feet were frozen. He sincerely hoped he'd be able to feel his feet again soon. The kerosene heater gave off a nice warm glow and steady heat.

He hadn't expected the trip to be so hazardous. He'd almost turned back three or four times. But with each mile he covered, the thought of seeing Gina spurred him on.

"Butch is confused and out of sorts. I left the carrier door open and the litter box and a water dish nearby with an old blanket he can curl up in." Gina looked at Ken's pale haggard face. His cheeks and chin were a deep mottled red and he shook a little as he hunched near the heater. "You look like you could use a cup of coffee."

"Great." Ken's feet and hands began to slowly warm. "Got anything to put in it?"

"Yes, as a matter of fact. I went to the liquor store and bought some Fra Angelica. I have a whole bottle. You can have as much as you want."

Ken smiled contentedly, sat back into the plush couch and stretched his feet closer to the heater. The heat felt so good, and very slowly he began to feel the tingle of blood flow in his extremities. But, more importantly, he was here with Gina. He was so glad to be here, even if he did almost kill himself by getting here. The important thing, the paramount thing was that he was safe, and he was with her.

Gina clattered about in the kitchen, using the ambient light from the lantern and heater to see what she was doing. It took a few minutes, but she located the mugs. Reaching the liqueur proved a little difficult. She found the stool with her shin, and reached the out----of----the----way cabinet.

Ken was really in her front room, sitting on her couch. It was hard to grasp, but the living proof was only a few feet away. How could he take his life in his hands and manage to climb that mountain to see her? Just to see her? It was foolhardy and crazy and she planned to chew him out about it as soon as he was feeling better.

Gina got all of the coffee things together. The hot water simmered madly away on the heater in the living room. Ken had pulled off his parka and boots and had leaned back on the couch with his eyes closed.

Gina leaned over him, looking deeply at the high chiseled cheekbones, and his ruddy cold----burnished face. His eyebrows and eyelashes were so dark they looked black. It still amazed her that her imagined Sir Ken was so like the painting on Ken's bedroom wall. Startling, unnerving, but very, very nice.

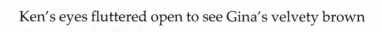

Ken's eyes fluttered open to see Gina's velvety brown ones staring at him.

"Here's your coffee. I put a bunch of the liqueur in it. I suppose a St. Bernard would do the same." She sat with him watching his hands shake with cold. She pulled his free hand to her, chafing it, alarmed at the icy feel of it. "You know you are one crazy man. I'd have been devastated if you'd gotten hurt... or worse. Should I ask how the roads were? Or should I stay in bliss---- filled ignorance?"

Ken slowly sipped his coffee, allowing the liqueur and Gina's chafing and the smoldering look in her eyes to warm his fingers and toes.

"I was very lucky. It's still so cold that very little ice had formed on the roads. I suffered with the cold, though. My car is not built for sub----zero temperatures. There are more drafts in that car than there are in your house."

"I'm so glad that you're in one piece. I had no idea that you'd come up that mountain with the snow coming down in buckets and the wind howling like a banshee. So," she said as she sat on the edge of the couch. She reached over and rubbed Colleen behind the ears. The dog's tail thumped merrily on the floor in counterpoint to the wind raging outside and pummeling the side of the house. "Why did you come?"

Ken put down his coffee and with excruciating slowness, reached over, and pulled Gina onto his lap. She smiled down at him as she pushed the lock of hair off his forehead.

"Because I wanted to take my chances and tell you that I love you," he said it simply.

Gina wrapped her arms around Ken's neck and held on. He loved her. He loved her and wanted to tell her so badly that he went up the silly mountain in the snow and ice. Gina's heartbeat thrummed with emotion, overwhelming emotion. And she loved him. She loved him from the first moment she saw those beautiful violet----blue eyes and that shaggy head of hair. Science and its denouncement of the impossibility of love at first sight could just take a hike.

She looked at him and then slowly lowering her mouth to his, kissed him deeply. She drew back and looked at his beautiful face for a long moment. "I love you, too. Just don't pull a stunt like that again. I'd miss you too much if you were gone."

Ken shut his eyes and inhaled deeply of kerosene heater, coffee, Fra Angelica, and the scent that was very much Gina. She loved him. It felt like he'd waited his whole life to hear those words, especially from someone as special as Gina. He kissed the top of her lovely head and the room started to feel perceptively warmer.

"Okay, I promise. I'm really, really tired." He yawned

hugely. "Do you think I can sleep on the floor?"

Gina kissed the tip of his nose. "Drink your coffee; I'll make you a pallet."

Gina hurried to her spare room and linen closet, grabbing all of the quilts, blankets, and pillows she could find. Butch greeted her entry into the spare room with a growl. "Deal with it, cat. You and Colleen are going to be BFFs before you know it."

When she returned to the living room, Ken had taken off a few more layers and hunched as close to the heater as he could.

"How're you doing?"

"Much better now that you've told me you love me. I would have had a lot of egg on my face if this relationship was a one----sided affair. But I didn't think it was. That's why I decided I had to try. I just had to get my brain out of the way of my heart enough to try." He looked at the heater and grinned. "We are never going to get rid of this heater, and when our great grandchildren ask us why, we will have quite a story to tell."

Gina laughed while she made up the fluffiest,

warmest bed with what she had available. "Do you realize that note in the ATM terminal advertising the heater was the first thing that brought us together? The heater was the bait. Maybe your Uncle Johann had the whole thing planned from the beginning."

"You know," said Ken as he crawled into the pallet and then held out his arms for Gina to join him. "As painful as it is for me to say, you are probably absolutely right." He rested his chin against Gina's head and sighed deeply, giving himself over to the good steady feel of her heartbeat, thinking of Gina, and his mother, and then of the crafty Uncle Johann. "Yeah, he's probably tuned into us right now, listening over his crystal ball."

Gina giggled and then sighed as Ken wrapped his arms around her and pulled her close. All of the fears, all of the constant doubts and worries, faded away on the sound of the wind.

Down the mountain in the city of Huntsville proper, Johann Glibmann poked at the fire, watching the sparks red and gold fly up into the darkened chimney, hovering and then disappearing. It had happened. He knew it had happened. The sparks glowed red hot as he poked the fire once again. They swirled about in the air, disappeared, and then came again, floating, hovering, like tiny, magic, red hot fairies. He thought about his family, his dear sister, now all gone. But like the sparks, the coals in the fireplace glowed red and hot, they didn't waver, they didn't diminish. Like the ever----

glowing coals, the new generation was here, steady, constant, the next in line to live and love. The steady burning coals were a symbol of love and hope.

About the Author

My father was a *Naval Aviator*, and my two brothers and I spent our youth and adolescence moving about every eighteen months. These moves were mostly around the South with one tour in Japan. The constantly changing environment meant that I had to make friends all over again each time we moved. That is a daunting task for anyone, especially a child, so a lot of my time I spent daydreaming and making up stories as well as changing the endings of the stories I was required to read in school.

I went to college to 'teach little kids how to sing on pitch,' and spent the following decades singing, teaching, and directing as well as teaching English and history in Middle school through junior college.

I write full time now, and live in central North Carolina with my husband and crazy dogs. I have four grown children and four grandchildren that I try to see as often as possible.

I'd love to hear from you. Please consider writing me a review and leaving it on Amazon on this book's page. You can reach me at **kathryn@scarboroughbooks.com**

Thanks

Author Notes

I lived in Huntsville, Al, home of the Marshall Space Flight Center and Redstone Arsenal and where many of the High Schools are named for Mercury Astronauts. Despite the fact that Huntsville is in Alabama, up in the mountains, the winters can sometimes be brutal. Hence, my idea of the catalyst of the kerosene heater for the story.

I hope you enjoy This Just In.... And as authors live and die by reviews, please leave a review on the book's Amazon page. You can see my other books at: **https://www.scarboroughbooks.com**. Feel free to write to me at **Kathryn@scarboroughbooks.com**

Made in the USA
Las Vegas, NV
12 August 2021

28068525R00152